THE MAN IN GREEN

PART ONE

MEDIEVAL FAIR

© Copyright 2006 Stan Phillips.

All rights reserved. No part of this publication may be reproduced, stored in a retrieval system, or transmitted, in any form or by any means, electronic, mechanical, photocopying, recording, or otherwise, without the written prior permission of the author.

Note for Librarians: A cataloguing record for this book is available from Library and Archives Canada at www.collectionscanada.ca/amicus/index-e.html
ISBN 1-4120-8637-x

Printed in Victoria, BC, Canada. Printed on paper with minimum 30% recycled fibre. Trafford's print shop runs on "green energy" from solar, wind and other environmentally-friendly power sources.

Offices in Canada, USA, Ireland and UK

Book sales for North America and international:
Trafford Publishing, 6E–2333 Government St.,
Victoria, BC V8T 4P4 CANADA
phone 250 383 6864 (toll-free 1 888 232 4444)
fax 250 383 6804; email to orders@trafford.com

Book sales in Europe:
Trafford Publishing (UK) Limited, 9 Park End Street, 2nd Floor
Oxford, UK OX1 1HH UNITED KINGDOM
phone 44 (0)1865 722 113 (local rate 0845 230 9601)
facsimile 44 (0)1865 722 868; info.uk@trafford.com

Order online at:
trafford.com/06-0393
10 9 8 7 6 5 4 3

THE MAN IN GREEN – MEDIEVAL FAIR

AND he was the man in green who was there long before the others had risen from their slumbers. He emerged from the green of the trees, but was somehow still half hidden by them. It was almost as if he were part of the forest. And in truth, he was.

A mystical ethereal being, his presence was unseen – almost unsuspected, as he flitted from tree to tree. But they knew he was there by the soft pad of his fairy footsteps in the woods or by his gentle breathing in the treetops. Half God he was and half hobgoblin, he filled a great part of the subconscious minds of the townspeople with his perpetuality, and though he abided with them, he was yet, apart from them. It was as if he were waiting for his time to come again.

For they had worshipped him once. Yes, in those far off days before the Romans had come with their strange Deities, they had danced and sang in the glades and clearings, tossing fruits and flowers as they thanked him for their crops, for their livestock and for their children. But then slowly over the years their prayers had become secretive, furtive. They began to come only at night, hiding in the shadows as they waited for the Moon to vanish behind the clouds before they came with their silent prayers and with their wounds. And he watched them and waited.

Later, after St. Augustine had come with his monks and his mysteries their worship changed again. It became guilt-ridden, sinful almost. It was as if they prayed with one eye always looking for a means of escape. And he watched them and waited. In time he became no more than a folk memory, an echo of the past. The only time they ever came close to him was when they touched wood for luck, or when they shivered slightly as they walked through his ancient clearings. And he endured, watching, waiting for that day when the new gods would become obsolete and the townspeople would need him again.

He inhabited the soul of the town, forgetting nothing, remembering all. Loving them, forgiving them for their neglect as he bided his time in the depths of the verdant trees. And he sighed as he watched them erecting their tents and stalls, his old eyes shifting endlessly as they registered each movement, his sharp ears heard every word and consigned them to the fathomless well of his mind. He was storing everything away against that day when they would come again to him with their prayers and their questions. And he must give them their answers. For he was the recorder. And he watched and waited.

The man in green who was there long before the others had risen from their slumbers.

THE TOWNSFOLK

AND they were the townsfolk in their reds and blacks and sombre browns. They were drifting to the fair in their ones and twos with a light of eager expectancy in their eyes. Some had come to sell their wares others had come to examine the produce of a competitor, and still more had come to just revel in the experience of a rare day of relaxation free from toil.

For most of them this annual, event had become like a small oasis of pleasure in a year of unrelieved hardship and struggle. This day, however, they were able to leave their fields and forges to peer in wonderment at the rare and exotic exhibitions that had been prepared for them. And they came to see the jousting, the acrobats, the midgets and the magicians. They came to hear the music and the song, to see the colours of the apparel of the wealthy, and to listen to the strange foreign tongue they still used for effect and privacy.

And the crowd grew and grew until the aisles between the overcrowded stalls were filled with a seething mass of bodies, and the air was filled with the mixed aromas of sweat and unwashed humanity blending with the odours of fruit and perfume. And they all jostled to obtain a better view, clinging to their children the while that they would not race off to find another, more exciting display. Laughing children, weeping children. Children with their eyes in perpetual motion as they attempted to escaped from the tight grasp of their equally awe-stricken parents.

MEDIEVAL FAIR

And the sun rose higher, warming the day. The noise grew, filling the air, assailing the senses. There was the preacher crying out against sin, and bodily excess while quenching his thirst from a pewter mug filled with ale. And he was competing for the crowd's attention with the raucous call of a tinker who banged a great ladle against the base of a mighty cooking-pot. And there was a woman in bright yellow raiment far outshining the plumage of the songbirds singing in their cages, as she squawked for the people to scrutinise her wares.

Then there was the neighing of half-terrified horses, the full-throated roar of the dancing bear, the frantic scream of a panic-stricken lost child. A sea of faces filled the day. Sights and sensations were carved upon the air. Till all at once it seemed to merge into one. It was as if the entire gathering had become a unity. An individual mighty creature that moved and breathed with its own singularity. A one-celled being that ebbed and flowed of its own will. And yet almost incredibly, there were spaces between them. That beast with its thousand faces was controlled by as many emotions, and in separating the parts from the whole, the unsuspecting onlooker could reveal layer upon layer of reality beyond comprehension. Unknown fears, lusts jealousies, needs, superstitions have been embroidered onto the fabric of the beast till it has become like a patchwork quilt of mortality, with each of its thousand faces hiding in its own way from the truth hidden within its single soul.

And they were the townsfolk in their reds and blacks and sombre browns.

THE HUNTER

THE man in green was a hunter armed with arrows of starlight.
And he stalked the essence of humankind
In the silent heart of the forest.
And the shaft that sped from his bow
Joined him to his target
That he was able to absorb and understand his prey.

THE MAN WITH THE DANCING BEAR

AND he was the man with the dancing bear, and together they had roamed the land from end to end. They would earn their bread in strange far-flung places as they performed in majestic turreted castles or outside dingy little inns. At fairs or at markets and sometimes alone beneath the skies they would dance and prance with joy. They had been together for so many years, growing older in each other's company. The man shared his food with the bear – when he had some, or shrugged fatalistically and starved a little. And beneath the cold and winter skies they would sleep together beneath the stars, with the warmth of the bear stilling the trembling of the shivering man.

But on the day of the fair, when they entered the small town, the sun was shining down from a clear blue sky. Brightly coloured tents stood proudly to greet them and flags and pennants fluttered in the gentle breeze. They found a small clearing and waited quietly until a puzzled expectant crowd had gathered about them, and then from the depths of his tattered cloak the man produced a tiny flute, which he placed between his lips. And all at once the sound filled the air, fresh and alive in the morning.

Slowly, slowly, the great brown bear began his dance, his mighty feet drumming in time to the merry tune. Then, as the pace of the music increased, his movements gathered speed. Faster he went and still faster as the man waved his flute before the mesmerised eyes of the bear. Round and round he went,

THE MAN IN GREEN

grunting a little with the effort, but somehow, almost human at the end of his rusting chain. And the man moved too, with his song rising and falling as he circled the bear.

The onlookers laughed and clapped with delight at the sight of the captive giant and his master. They shouted for more and tossed their few coins into the man's shabby bonnet. But the performers heard them not for their world was filled with music and dance. And their world was filled with something else, it was more than dependence, more than love. It was perhaps a question of freedom and captivity, for did not the chain that held the bear more tightly entrap the man. And the day wore on, the music becoming no more than a faint echo upon the still evening air. And they wandered off together, the man and the bear, with their shadows growing long in the fading sun. To disappear into memory over the brow of the hill. And who was left behind to comprehend the sheer bliss of the man with naught but his flute, his music and the long dusty road that stretched ahead.

And he was the man with the dancing bear who roamed the land from end to end.

THE WIZARD

AND he was the wizard with his wagon of wonder. Brightly painted it was, with its crescent moons and comets and stars. It was covered with symbols of magical mystery, and drawn by a prancing horse of purest white. He sat up upon his perch and toyed with his gold braided reins as he allowed his horse to find a clear spot for the performance. And he looked at the crowd with eyes that were the colour of his cape, black and flecked with grey, filled with secrets and lost, hidden knowledge. His head was topped with a conical cap of silver which reflected the rays of the brilliant sun.

At last when his horse had stopped and was quietly grazing at a small patch of grass, he descended slowly from his wagon and stood silently, majestically, watching the curious, simple country folk as they gathered before him. Then suddenly he raised his wrinkled hands above his head and produced a blazing wand from the empty air. And it sparked with the colours of the rainbow as he waved it to and fro. The crowd gasped in astonishment and stepped back as the magician was engulfed in a sea of crimson smoke that turned to blue and back again. Then from within the depths of the kaleidoscopic steam, he moved like lightening, he conjured white doves, scampering rabbits. Coloured rain fell upon flowers that blossomed in fiery embers and he turned water into wine. The superstitious onlookers prayed with their eyes wide and their mouths agape, but they would not, could not, leave.

THE MAN IN GREEN

What, they were wondering, would this magical man do next? And he ate the fire, which became a stream of pennants which he drew from his mouth in a never-ending stream. Afterwards he sat with them upon the grass and told fortunes, he looked into their palms and read the lines therein, he peered into the murky depths of the crystal and spoke to them of love, life, fat pigs and abundant harvests. He told of travels and homecomings and of peaceful death in hearty old age. And they sighed and wept and laughed at his tidings. Then he told them stories of strange lands beyond the seas and they listened enthralled as he spoke of elephants and tigers, pyramids and fiery oceans.

"I have been and I have seen where the sun never sets,
Where the clouds are still in the sky.
Where the mountains breathe flames to explode in the night,
And belief is suspended in time".

And he sighed as he looked at their eager faces.

"More, more!" they demanded.

So he told them of armies filled with one-breasted women, of strange painted caverns and mystical walled cities filled with treasures beyond comprehension. And he sighed at their child-like innocence as they clapped and laughed about him. For he knew that he would never see them again, he knew that as he went from the Fair in the fading light of day, he would never return.

For hidden within that deep well of secrets, there was one of which he could never speak. It was like a tiny bell ringing with a muffled knell within the deepest recesses of his mind.

Was it an echo of a fragment of his memory? A relic of the past, perhaps? Or a strange backwards recollection of that which was still to be? Or was it a far memory of time out of mind, of time unlived? Or was it a memory of a dream so real it could almost be touched, felt, sensed? Whatever it was, he knew that his magic would be lost in the debris of history. His art would be buried in the sands of time. His destiny was to be the stake and he could almost smell the acrid smoke filling his nostrils. And he smiled a little at the thought. The wizard with his wagon of wonder.

THE CRONE

AND she was the crone in her garment of grey. Old and bent with her twisted nose and crooked back. Prodigiously ugly, with her sparse hair, grey as her dress. Crawling lice cavorted beneath her black bonnet which was pulled forward over her tiny, darting eyes. Her stick went tap-tap on the cobbles before her, and small children fled her path crying "Witch, witch!" And older folk averted their eyes, crossing themselves for grace. She bore her wares upon her back in a sack of patches and called out in a quavering voice,

> "Who will buy my fine cambrics?" she cried, "fit they are for a fine lady. And buttons and ribbons I have a'plenty, who will buy?"

But they passed her by as if she were not there. And the morning sun was hot upon her and the day that stretched ahead seemed to have no end. She rested in the shade of a tree with her effects surrounding her and gnawed on an aged crust of bread.

She was watching the multitude as they danced and sang, making merry in the warmth of the late summer day, but yet it was only one small part of her that saw the merry-making. Those ancient eyes were focused instead upon other days. They could see beyond the fair, beyond the pain and tiredness to another time, a youthful, gay time when there had been no suffering. To a world where she too had danced in the sunshine, singing her joy for all to hear, a world wherein she had worn her youth like a shining medallion, and her hair had gleamed then, as black as the midnight sky bathed in moonlight.

And she too had known love in those far off days. Her awakening body had responded willingly to the touch of an ardent hand. And the warmth and heat in those days had not been oppressive. Her wrinkled frame trembled as she recalled that gentle touch. Shivered at the recollection of her long dead lover's kiss. She was not called 'witch' then. And children ran not from her. And the trees seemed greener then, the skies bluer. And the aching loneliness washed over her as a tear started in a glazed eye sunken in the shell of her face. And she was unaware of the passing brown dog which nuzzled her cheek.

"Cambrics", she croaked, "who will buy my fine cambrics?"

Later they found her lying there. She was still and at peace, with a faint tear stain etched upon her face. And they buried her there, beneath the soil beneath the tree, with a small wooden cross being all there was to show the passing of

The crone in her garment of grey.

THE FISHERMAN

THE man in green was a fisherman.
  Casting his nets in an endless sweep of the oceans.
And he stored everything he caught against the day of need.
  It was the quintessence of mortals for which he fished.
  Not the sophisticated layers of lies and half truths.
  And he smiled as he peeled away the veneers of falsehood to reveal the
  Potential of the race.

THE SIMPLETON

HE was the simpleton with the mind of a child. His crooked mouth with its rotted teeth was a gash in his face. Spittle stains and spilled food marred further his already foul clothing. And they mocked his shambling gait, laughed at his ungainly manner. Mothers snatched mischievous children from his wavering path, while the menfolk cursed him as he limped clumsily past them.

He was a solitary man, and they treated him like a sideshow, or they ignored him. But he answered their scorn with a strange lopsided smile. Fools that they were, for they did not comprehend that private place that existed behind his ruined brain. That unique land where he alone could dwell. It was a magical country where great caverns of gold were washed by silver waters. A hidden world where trees grew tall and straight, and were tended only by the gentle hand of God. And the sky was filled with bright stars set in the black velvet canopy of the night. And he could touch them. Yes, he could reach out his hand and move them in the firmament, shifting Time and Space as he willed, forming complex patterns upon the endless canvas of the universe.

And the air was filled with the scent of enchantment and the colours of delight. Vast, vast was the world within his shattered mind, filled with mighty mountains, deep canyons. And inhabited by love. And his soul was without a stain. His life without sin. That cursed, scorned, reviled man.

Who was the simpleton with the mind of a child.

THE LOVERS

AND they were the lovers with stars in their eyes, for whom time had stood still. Their laughter rang in the sky, sang in the sky with the jubilant birds. And their silences caused the day to hold its breath. They ran through the woods with the sounds of the Fair dimly echoing in their ears. They saw naught but each other and heard only the sounds of the beating of their entwined hearts.

A maid of sixteen she was, and she wore her love as if she were a princess in her crimson gown. And her hair was of shimmering gold which turned to flame in the endless sun. He, in his turn, was a youth of eighteen. A young man destined soon for the wars. And he wore his destiny like a cape of pride. How would he fare in the mud and the blood of battle? Was he to return with his limbs and his life intact, or would he instead lie rotting in a hasty grave? And would the maiden weep her young dreams away amid the falling leaves of passing Summer.

It was all in the future. Now was all they possessed. Tomorrow's fears were unspoken, unheeded, as they lay still in the long ripening corn and watched the hawk swooping down upon its unsuspecting prey. And they clung to each other in a kiss filled with all passion and emotion of unfulfilled adolescence. Their bodies came to life within the framework of that endless kiss, and they grasped each other in a mad urgent need.

Holding, caressing, until they at last lay naked beneath the hot sun. And he looked into her smiling eyes which he closed with a kiss, and then he rested his tousled head upon her soft breasts. Shutting his own eyes at the ecstasy of the warmth of her.

Tired sleeping arms entwining.
Time passing.
Night falling.
Stars shining.
Day ending.

An eternity of love compressed into a single consummation. And they would remember the day of the Fair forever, come what may.

The lovers with stars in their eyes for whom time had stood still.

THE ROBBER

AND he was Will, the cutpurse with his helter skelter hands. He walked through the fair munching an apple, red and juicy, that he had purloined from the tray of a passing pedlar. And his darting blue eyes flashed here and there, never still as they searched for a likely target.

A trinket or a coin

Would very shortly join

The stack of treasure hidden in his coat

And the hat he wore so decorously upon his head, still felt warm from its previous owner.

He watched the passing parade, fair maidens with their rings and brooches, and he assessed the damsels for their worth rather than their charm. And he winked at them and smiled as he passed a few pleasant moments in their company and he praised their beauty as he removed a small memento from their person. And he discussed long and loud with the men, telling ribald tales, or learnedly discoursing about crops and husbandry as his long fluttering fingers explored the depths of their capes. And then he was gone like a will-o-the-wisp, his mocking laughter echoing on the summer air. but within that laughter there dwelt a strange sadness, for all his stolen valuable brought him little joy, and there was always a hidden fear in his eyes as he constantly watched for pursuit. And the hair on the back of his neck still stood on end at the recollection of the horror of the hue and cry that had tormented him for days.

MEDIEVAL FAIR

Later in the day, when he sat alone beneath a tree calculating the value of his day's efforts, he watched the fire burning behind the white gathering clouds, and wondered how soon it would be for him to take his turn hanging from a tree, rather than sitting beneath one. And he wondered whether he would still smile as he dangled there in the pale light of the setting sun. Will, the cutpurse with his helter-skelter hands.

THE SOLDIER

AND he was the soldier returned from the Holy Land. He stood half a head taller than the average man, and the women turned to watch him as he walked slowly through the crowd, so fair of face was he. And the men envied him for his strength and majestic carriage. But he saw them not, neither did he heed their calls of welcome and their shouts of approval. For his mind was still at the battles and his clear but troubled eyes saw naught but the fields of war with its bleeding horses and its broken men. And the cries of the dying were still echoing within his wounded head.

He had wanted to be a priest, but because of his size and power, they had made him an unwilling warrior. When younger, he had attempted in words of sweet simplicity, to reveal the Word of God upon the altar stone of creation. But he had found nobody who could understand simplicity. And in deeds of perfect humility he had tried to assuage the pains of the living. But had found none to comprehend humility. He had, within a framework of unsullied love, attempted to lay the souls of men before the throne of the Lord. But no-one had the ability to perceive love. And he watched as his world continued to revolve in its cycle, looking out into the never-ending depths of timeless space weeping for its children.

Watching as they strove to extricate themselves from the claws of chaos as they drank of the milk that flowed unchecked from the udders of disaster. And the soldier sat awhile and accepted the mug of ale that a well-wisher had thrust into his

MEDIEVAL FAIR

great hand. Soon a small motley crowd had gathered about him, but he hardly knew they were there.

"Tell us a tale of the wars", asked one of their number. He looked up at the speaker and smiled wearily, before he spoke, more to himself than to his audience.

"I have seen them running, running on feet of quicksilver with the wind in their streaming hair. And they were trampling helpless children with their frantic flying footsteps. A castle is burning, it is a strange dreamlike fire, and it is coming closer and closer, soon it will reach the town and the flames will engulf us all. The whole crumbling edifice will soon explode and the fleeing horde will perish in the cataclysm. And still they run, thundering feet unable to avoid the falling fiery buildings. And crushed bodies putrefy upon the baking streets".

He took a breath and supped some of his ale and looked up to find he was alone. He shrugged and continued.

"The city is aflame, red beacons are lighting up the sky, the birds are flying high in the heavens to escape the destruction, and the river boils beneath them. And still the people run, soundless screams are etched on parched faces. The agony goes on and on. And still they run. But I cannot escape, I stand as if transfixed in the fires of my own terror as I watch the flames come ever nearer. Charred buildings are standing starkly against the magic of my dreams as a million people seem to rush by me, turning me this way and that in a weird dance of death. And shaking like a leaf I watch as the multitude vanish into the acrid smoke. And the flames are licking at my feet.

Slowly I watch as my body becomes a pyre and I am unable to run from my fears. I am suddenly become the total of all my nightmares and I can observe my ashes as they blow through the barren windswept land to vanish from my sight. They will disappear as those fears for which I died will disappear, will cease to be as I shall cease to be. And my soul will shake his head and wonder why. And the souls of everyman will weep and wonder why. And God will wring His hands in despair as He turns from us to go into the immeasurable night".

The soldier dropped his mug to the ground, spilling the contents on to the dry grass. And buried his face in his hands. The man who was the soldier back from the Holy Land.

THE SPIDER

THE man in the mantle of green was a spider.
    And he spun his web of gossamer
To entrap the souls of men in its gentle yielding strands.
And he consumed their minds, not their bodies, in his endless search for truth and knowledge.
And he released them with their hearts filled with longing.
With a small question burned onto their spirit.

THE TROUBADOUR

AND he was the troubadour with his songs of love. He had journeyed far in his brightly coloured raiment to be at the fair, and he had sung his heart out on the road for all who cared to listen. On dark nights with moon riding high above the scudding clouds, he was to be heard singing at the gate of the Baron's castle. Thus he could gain his entrance, and perhaps a crust of bread. And his sweet voice seemed to rise even higher than the clouds, to dance in the sky with the sparkling stars, and then at other times he would be found singing within the walls of murky taverns, with a tankard in one hand and a morsel of food in the other. But the songs were always the same.

He would sing of love, to inflame the passions of his listeners. Or he would regale them with loud brave songs of battle, that told of heroic deeds to stir the blood. And he knew soft lullabies, gentle caressing carols that would move his audience to sleep, as he drifted silently from them with a full belly and a chinking purse. But it was of love that he sang best of all, and sometimes the fires of the young or the memories of the aged would move him so much that his own loins would yearn for relief. Would ache for the soft touch of a woman's hand. And he would seek out a serving maid or a tavern wench, and would make such exquisite love, that afterwards they would be moved to tell him that his talent for song was exceeded only by his gift for romance.

MEDIEVAL FAIR

On the day of the Fair he wandered through the crowd with his checkered cap awry upon his unruly hair. There was the usual excited gleam in his tawny eyes as he watched them as they bustled by, and he stood awhile, quietly waiting with his lute hung loosely from his shoulder.

"Who shall listen to my song?" he cried, "a song of the fair or a song for the fairest. A few coins in my cap will bring you an hour of delight". And they laughed as they threw a few small pennies to him. He sang then, his vibrant young voice rising above the cacophony around him, and seeming to silence them all, so compelling was the sound of his song. His music was about the day, about the wine they would drink and of the food they would eat, of the games they would play and of the love they would make at the end of the day when they would lie content on their beds, or perhaps in some quiet hayrick, far from prying eyes.

His song was of sunshine, starlight and joy. It was also of the good God who watched over them, keeping them safe, and their children free from harm. And much later when his song was ended, the fair over, and his audience had long gone on their way, his voice still seemed to echo around the deserted field. And he wondered as he lay entwined in the arms of a gentle, willing maid. Would anyone remember him? Would they remember his song when they awoke to a new day? And would they perhaps, say a small prayer for him? And he sighed as he looked out into the night, before embracing his sweet companion for just one last time. The troubadour with his songs of love.

THE GIRL

SHE was the girl in the gown of brilliant white. And in the dim mist of early morning, dew dappled day, she walked through the silent sylvan trees. So softly did she tread that naught was disturbed by her presence, no leaf nor blade of grass was moved by her gentle footsteps. There was a holiness in the glade, a peaceful throbbing in the throat of creation. Suddenly the girl paused, seeming to wait with her head tilted to the side, her golden hair cascading about her shoulders. Then, as if by magic, a bird alighted upon her outstretched arm. It rested quietly for a moment. Coloured brightly like a rainbow with its reds and yellows and blues and greens. Then it began to sing its new song of awakening day. And the voice of the bird rejoiced in the mellow depths of the listening forest. Joy for the dawn, joy for the new life of the morning. Joy for the song, and joy for the ability to create it. And greatest joy for the pure being of the song.

The girl smiled at the bird and began her own song, without words, soaring high above the tree-tops that swayed in the rhythm of her music. The bird had fallen silent as it listened keenly to her. It looked up into her eyes and flew away. It filled the sky with the colour of its jewel bedecked wings which seemed to grow great in the music. It moved gracefully upon the air currents, it swooped, banked, climbed and vanished into the west.

The girl in brilliant white fell silent as she watched the bird disappear in a blaze of dazzling sunlight, and tears gathered in the depths of her great glistening eyes. There were tears for the transient bird. Tears for the faded song. But they were of no avail, for the bird did not return to her, and the tears fell over her cheeks to descend as droplets of dewdamp silver weeping upon her breast. And she buried her fair face in her hands and sobbed for the bird and for the song which had fled with the dawn.

At the end of the long day, the girl in white lay herself down upon a soft pillow of leaves, her slumbers barely disturbed by the sounds of the resting, rustling forest which shifted ceaselessly about her, till she woke again to yet another golden morning. To walk again through the flowering verdure as she waited the coming of the kaleidoscope bird which came to her each day summoned by the beauty of the breaking waking morn.

Till the girl in white
Puts the bird to flight
With her own uninhibited exuberance
And she lived her life apart, lonely but never alone.
The girl in the gown of brilliant white.

THE OWL

THE man in green was an owl
And he sat, apparently motionless, in the tree tops

His eyes, though, were never still as they searched the faces of the crowd.

And his pointed ears were constantly moving as they detected every shifting sound that was wafted upwards.

He was like a leech as he assimilated sights and sensations.

Absorbing them into his soul,

Before he spread his majestic wings and flew off into the forest.

THE JUGGLER

And there stood Mark the juggler with his clubs of coloured lightning. First two, then three, four, five, six are tossed in the air, and his hands are a blur as he moves forward, back, left and right. Catching them with apparent ease and hurling them high up into the still morning. People stop and watch bemused to see the clubs soaring over Mark's head. But he did not see them as they stood before him, for his mind was concentrated only on to the performance of his small miracle.

Red, blue, gold and green clubs marvellously merging. "Ooh!" and "Ahh!" went the small crowd. But they spoke and clapped quietly so as not to disturb the remarkable young man. And they left little in his cap, afraid that their movements would destroy his feat. And they did not see the tiny tear in the corner of his eye, the tear that told of his awareness of the easy boredom of the crowd who would soon tire of his tricks and walk off with scarcely a backward glance. Leaving him alone with the silence, and perhaps enough to buy himself a jug of wine or a few morsels of food. And he thought to himself, that possibly, in the morning, some small child might come and stand where he stood, and toss a few apples in the air, and in his attempts to catch them, might just imagine that he was

Mark the juggler with his clubs of coloured lightning.

THE MUMMER

And he was the mummer with a thousand faces. Beguiling and mystical he strutted in his chequered costumer upon his small stage and changed the world about him. He appeared to possess a million different voices as he called out stridently. And he could create a new scene with the merest shrug of his shoulder or by the lifting of one eyebrow. They held their breath as they watched lest they should miss some part of his drama, and they strained their ears to catch every cadence of his constantly changing speech.

One moment he was Christ, bleeding upon His lonely cross, and so real was his interpretation, that even the sky seemed to darken in eternal anger. Then he became a thousand shouting, swearing, singing soldiers marching to violent victorious war. And the crowd felt as if they were part of the battle. It was as if they could smell the horses sweating amid the blood and the pain of conflict. Afterwards he became the lovers crooning beneath the oaks of Autumn, and he wept and grieved, sighed and laughed as he encapsulated for one brief moment all the anguish of unrequited love, or all the joy of fulfilment touching a half-forgotten memory that dwelt within the hearts of his captivated audience. And the birds fell silent in the presence of the mummer. And the air was filled with wonder.

Later when he walked wearily and alone from the empty fairground, he watched the passing clouds rimmed with gold from the rays of the setting sun, and he was filled with such unutterable joy that he felt his heart would burst. And he was the receptacle of all mankind, yet he was unknown as he changed the world about him.

The mummer with a thousand faces.

THE CAT

THE man in green was a cat skulking in the alleys
    And sliding down the rooftops.

His endlessly shifting eyes missing nothing in the shadows of the moon.

He saw them at their worst during the long nights.

He watched them as they robbed, raped, killed and wept.

And he arched his back, filling the air with his raucous squeals of grief.

And he fled with the curses of man echoing in his ears.

THE TUMBLERS

THE tumblers came leaping, rolling down the hill.
   Over and over in their multicoloured costumes.
Bells ringing,
Feet flying,
Up and over.
Now on their hands,
Now on their heads
Whooping,
Shouting,
One high,
Two high,
Three high,
Four high.
Up and over,
Round and round.
Leap frogging,
Cart wheeling.
In the air,
On the ground.
Up and over,
Falling, falling
Rolling, rolling.

And they raced off into the distance, to become no more than a blur of frantic colour, as they vanished as swiftly as they came. The tumblers who came leaping and rolling down the hill.

THE DWARF

AND he was the dwarf with a countenance of beauty. He had journeyed from far away on stunted little legs that carried him, filled him with pain, along endless roads and over rutted fields. Strange lands, strange languages had filled his life till he had arrived, by chance, upon this bright and noisy fairground. He sat upon the grass, breathing heavily with the effort of his travels. His sad eyes were set like sparkling gems, brilliant diamonds shining in the depths of his lined face. His beard, once black, was now ash grey, and there was an air of doomed sorrow about him as he placed his black cap upon his head, rose unsteadily to his feet and limped away from the fair.

Unseen.

Unheeded.

Unwanted.

If only they had seen him as he passed briefly among them.

If only they could have explored the soul of him.

For he was a man of wondrous character,

A man of mischievous devilry.

One who could love those who despised him, could respect those that disagreed with him.

And he could forget his pain in laughter.

The world would be grieving his passing yet,

If the world had only been aware of his existence.

If only they could have seen him,

Yuri, the dwarf with the countenance of beauty.

THE MONEYLENDER

AND he was Abraham the moneylender in his cloak of black and braided gold. He had ridden into the throng upon an ancient donkey with a satchel of coins strapped to his back. And he surveyed the multitude with an experienced eye, weighing them up, trying to guess which of them would need his services during the ensuring hours. He would lend them money at such usurious rates that they would curse him at repayment time, but he had seen so much of his hard earned wealth vanish into the coffers of the mighty, never to return, that he felt justified in penalising the lowly for the profligacy of their betters.

And both sections of the community reviled him for his money. And for the large cool house he had built in the town, with its airy rooms, its draperies and fountains. And they envied him his wine and the fruit he imported from Iberia. They desired his beautiful but untouchable daughters. But most of all they hated him for their need of him. For the grinding penurious taxes and the unwinnable wars that created the market place he inhabited. And they spat at his retreating back as surely as they had smiled at his approach.

Sometimes he wondered, as he sat upon his stool with his books and ledgers on the ground beside him, 'Who is the alien?' Was it him with his outlandishly ornamented garb, with his garish capes and the tasselled crimson skullcap that adorned his head at all times? Or was it perhaps them, with their strange, almost primitive superstitions? And a small bitter

THE MAN IN GREEN

smile twisted his lips as he fondled his long beard. Their world, he thought, was bounded by the distance they could travel in a day, they were imprisoned by the invisible walls of the shire in which they dwelt. And they had been drawn together by an unseen intangible cord, intermarrying, interbreeding, so that they all eventually, came to look alike with only the addition of 'son' at the end of a name distinguishing father from his child.

And they shared the same fears of death, sin and poverty. Their eyes, too, were never still when they spoke, almost as if they were afraid that their souls could be seen through them. But, on the other hand, thought Abraham, am I not subject to those same fears. Does not death fill me with terror? No, he answered himself, my passage through this life has been filled with death. I can look upon its face without trepidation and greet its welcoming arms with a kind of relief when it beckons my aging bones to its temple.

The pain of dying, though, perhaps that frightens me a little. But there again I have experienced so much torment, that surely the relief and the glory that is mine after the agony is ended is to be eagerly anticipated. And what of sin, he speculated, I have always attempted to live within the ancient laws of my people, and on those occasions when I have veered from the path, I have atoned for my actions as best I could. Still, he smiled a little, they are always inventing new sins for the Jews to fly in the face of – maybe I have missed one or two, never mind, I will apologise to God when the time comes.

And what of poverty, he continued, ah I have been poor so often in the past that I shall not fret about it. And he waved a disparaging arm in the air, almost knocking to the ground an elderly pedlar who happened to be passing by at such an inopportune moment. Abraham chuckled to himself, of course, poverty will upset my daughters more than a little, but soon I shall find them rich husbands, and thereby solve that problem. But supposing I did lose it all, what would I do? He shrugged his shoulders, I would do what Jews always do, pack up and move on. But where to, where was there left for them to go? And in his mind's eye he retravelled the long road that had brought him to this place, to sit upon his stool in the midday sun, philosophising in the heat of the day.

There had been times in the past, he recalled, when he had sat in the airy palaces of the caliphs of the East, sipping iced lemon from golden goblets with the cooling winds of the desert blowing through the decorated windows. And they had sought his advice on matters financial, and they in turn had told him of their medicine, taught him their mathematics, shown him their art, and let him share in their scientific experiments. And even years after, he could still revel in the sensuous visions created by their poetry.

Those were the heady days, the happy days before the Crusaders had come again, bringing with them their wagons of war and their strange violent faith. And Abraham had been taken with all the other Jews and had been squeezed like a nut between the opposing jaws of the Christian and Saracen armies, until everything had been extracted, money, land, blood and hope. They had taken it all, leaving the Jews to pack up what was left, and continue their eternal journey to the promised land.

THE MAN IN GREEN

For Abraham, the trek took him along the great North African coast. He passed through Alexandria in what was to become the mighty empire of the Mamalukes. On across the burning sands to Tripoli, through the lands of the Almohads, and then over the waters from Tangiers to Iberia. And he rested a while in Spain, gathering unto himself riches, knowledge and family responsibility. He had been happy in that warm hot-blooded land until the evil head of the beast of racial envy raised its gruesome head once more. Sending him on his way again, leaving behind the white, brilliant castles of Granada, and the kingdoms of Aragon, Navarre and Castille. Then on through France with everything that had gone before becoming no more than a hazy, misty memory of pain and luxury.

And he felt as if each step he took was taking his further into barbarism. It was as if each border he crossed was a veneer being stripped off the thin layers of the bright arrogant civilisations of the East. And he wept with the fear of all the unknown lands that lay between him and his salvation. And on the day of the Fair, as he sat pondering the present and remembering the past, his thoughts turned to the future. For word had been sent to him that a new edict was soon to be passed banishing all Jews from the land, to be sent once more into unwilling exile, and his old eyes filled with tears at the thought.

But where, the thought again, where can we go? Europe and the Middle East were still not safe for the Children of Israel, and probably never would be so. And he flung his thoughts wider and wider still, examining and rejecting options as he did so. Till suddenly and joyfully he clapped his wrinkled hands and shouted aloud. "Cathay, Cathay!" and he coughed to hide his embarrassment as they all stared at him. Cathay – he rolled the magical word around in his mind, recalling how they had spoken of it as they had lolled on the sumptuous cushions amid the marble mosaics of Morocco. They had talked almost reverently of that great mysterious land, far, far away to the east. With its cities as old as time, with its wealth and wisdom, its birds and trees and flowers, its art and music, and perfumes that could make the head reel.

But how, he considered solemnly, can we ever get there? How on earth could we ever contemplate crossing Europe with its plagues and wars, and then again, what about the Inquisition? And he shivered at the thought of that infant abomination slowly opening its monstrous maw, to plunge the world into new paroxysms of terror and torment. And the thought of Cathay began to recede as he imagined the ills that could befall his family on the long and arduous journey. But then suddenly there was an idea being created within his brain, it was like a small itch, and if he could only scratch away the surface perhaps he could reveal what lay hidden. He furrowed his aged brow till it came. And the idea exploded within his mind filling him with new hope, fervour and fresh ambition.

"I shall not travel to the East, I shall go to the West", he shouted aloud, surprising the populace with the vehemence of this outburst, but he paid them no heed as his mind worked furiously recalling the youthful discussions in which he had taken part. How the Arabian scholars had taught him the great heresy of the spherical world, and how they had proved it to him with their maps, charts and strange algebraic symbols. And perhaps, he considered further, the risks would be less than staying where the threat of death hung over them all like a disease. And he rose to his feet scattering his books and papers to the ground as he did so, but keeping a tight hold on to his money bag as he hurried away from the Fair oblivious to the puzzled stares that followed his retreating back, and to the strange reaction to his thoughts which had become a spoken monologue.

"I shall build me a boat, a great ship big enough to take me and mine away from this accursed continent, and across the unknown seas to Cathay, we shall leave it all behind, all the fear and famine, all the shame and sorrow, and we will search for peace in that mighty land to the East that is really to the West". And he laughed as he went to his great new adventure. And the onlookers tapped their foreheads to mock his insanity. But they never saw him again, and those that owed him money rejoiced, while the others who needed his wealth were sorrowful, all of them however, often wondered what ever became of

Abraham the moneylender in his cloak of black and braided gold.

THE POET

THE main in green was a poet,
    And his words are spoken in hushed whispers
By the winds of Autumn.
In the depths of despair they can be heard, soothing,
In the biting gales of the white winter.
And in the glory of the blazing summer
They are sung by the birds in the trees
Or by the lover inspired by the urgency of passion.
But it is the infant Spring that speaks his words best of all,
    Telling of rebirth, of new life awakening
    With a smile and a promise.

THE HARLOT

SHE was the woman without a name, a vessel filled with empty promises. As she paraded wantonly past the brightly caparisoned tents with her painted face and her vacant eyes, she smiled her welcome to the passing men and boys. And for some, her full body and her experienced hands gave a brief lustful sense of relief. And she would leave them lying there with their glassy eyes and empty purses to reflect, as all men do, of the speedy devaluation of the act of coupling, to wonder how it should be that one moment you would give all you possess for that short clandestine burst of illicit satisfaction, and then when it is all over, you are left with guilt, recrimination and very little else.

And the harlot? She has merely smoothed down her dress and gone on her way to search for another client. She was both young and old at the same time, her dreams were filled with the memory of hot breath and clawing fingers, and her eyes were waiting to shed a million unspilled tears. Tears for the happy child who had played once in the winter snow, or run merrily beneath the rich red trees of Autumn. They had called her Mary then, and had taught her of God and His commandments. About Jesus and His mother for whom she had been named. She, in turn, had learned well and willingly. The promises she had given then had not been empty. And the smallholding where she had lived was filled with toil, joy and reward.

MEDIEVAL FAIR

Then, one sad day, the soldiers had come to collect the unpaid taxes, and they came with their swords and fire to lay it to waste in one short afternoon with their killing and their raping. Mary had been left for dead with the corpses of her family, the unwilling receptacle of the seed of a dozen frantic, furious yeomen, left for dead with the embryo of an unwanted, doomed infant implanted within her thirteen-year-old womb. And between her tightly clenched teeth was the lobe of an ear, bitten off in her blind panic. And even eight years later, as she promenaded sensuously through the peasantry and nobility, she could still taste it, bitter and raw, as the alien blood had dried upon her lips. And the memory was like a cancer eating away at her. But she plied her trade with a smile, for deep in her heart she knew that one day a man would lower himself upon her, a man with a mutilated ear, who was fated to die in revenge for her mutilated soul. And she was searching for him, high and low.

The woman without a name who was a vessel filled with empty promises.

THE MAN IN GREEN

AND he was the man in green, and it was he that remained when the others had long gone to their slumbers. And it was he that prowled the night where the Fair had been, and his memories are etched into ours. It was the man in the mantle of green who subtly changed the fairground, so that ever after, there would remain a taste of it on the wind, a smell of it in the air. And in the atmosphere there would always be the faintest touch of the grief and the glory of the day. And he passed like a silent ghost, where the bright tents had stood so proudly in the sun. And he laughed again at the recollection of the tumblers' racing antics, and his laughter echoed on the night to become a magical engraving on time. Stark night, dark night, dim stars half lighting the spot where the young lovers had poured out their anguished love in a precious moment, filled with urgency. And where the whore had lain with her consorts as she followed her destiny.

The main in green passed again the clearing where the bear had cavorted, and he whistled its prancing song, and recalled its shuffling gait and strange dignity in the hot sun. Then he lay awhile on the hillside where the mummer had acted out his remarkable plays, and the passion stirred him again, filling his soul with longing. There had been so much at the Fair, but it was only the man in green who could remember the very little things.

He would recall the colour of the grass. The blue of the sky. The song of the birds. He would remember the weeping children. The bizarre duet of the girl in brilliant white and her kaleidoscopic bird. And he would treasure the kiss he had placed upon the ever sleeping eyes of the dead crone. And the lined, travel weary, pain filled face of the dwarf was carved by the man in green onto the trunks of the trees in the woods. For he was the recorder, and nobody knew where he had passed. But he has taken their forgotten memories unto himself and painted them onto the windows of Eternity.

And if we look very hard, we can just see the remnant of his shadow in the moonlight. And we can tell where he has been. And perhaps where he still remains. For he is the recorder, and he abides. The man in green who remained when the others had long gone to their slumbers.

THE MAN IN GREEN

PART TWO

REFLECTIONS OF THE FAIR

REFLECTIONS OF THE FAIR

THE MAN IN GREEN

AND he was the man in green who watched silently as the world became middle aged and mellow. Like a sentinel he had observed the centuries drifting by. Filled with smiles and filled with weeping. Fire and famine had wafted past him on the winds of the fleet-footed years. And he had seen them all, laden with grief and pain. With birth and recreation. All in their turn as a part of the endlessly altering landscape. There were always fresh faces to memorise, new souls to be absorbed into his. And he wondered constantly, at the infinity of them all. And he witnessed them, as they came fresh and pristine and innocent into the world as babes, and he filled the skies with an echo of their childish laughter, and wept with them as they shed their tears.

And he watched them too, as they grew from the purity of their childhood into the unruly chaos of their maturity. And wished the while that he could take them, could shape, could guide them to the fulfilment of their capabilities. But he knew all along that the desire for stability, for competence, for love must issue from them and not his influence.

And he watched them as the shadows of passing time crept upon them, corroding their souls, confusing their needs with each passing year. And he cried out in his impotence as they journeyed down the stumbling passages of their lives. One day, he told himself, one day. And he shrouded himself in his garment of greenery concealed in the heart of the trees and watched. Watched and noted the shifting clouds, the rising and setting sun, the ebbing tides that marked the wandering of the years. And the tears that flowed from his venerable heart were a stain upon a flawed creation that he was powerless to change.

Yet.

Yet.

And he clung to that word as a shipwrecked sailor clutches at driftwood. One day, he said again, one day. And the leaves above him sighed in the breeze, whispered a small prayer of consolation. For they knew him, believed in him, had faith in the man in green who watched silently as the world became middle-aged and mellow.

THE PEOPLE

AND they were the people in their frocks and smocks and fashionable finery. Like children they had gathered to line the wayside and watch the circus procession. To stand and wait beneath the cloudless sky till the performers paraded by. Dandies in blue and reds with silver topped canes and powdered hair. Ladies in bonnets and bows with silken purses and painted faces. Fat farmers with staff and gaiters a mopping their foreheads. And their wives patiently alongside them, watching each other. And their young ones too, from youngest to eldest, red faced with expectancy, munching on homemade gingerbread chattering wildly. Like a forest they all were as they swayed to and fro. Glowing with colour constantly changing in the radiance of the bright eyed sun.

And like a forest there was a multiplicity of fragrances upon the air. But instead of the aroma of leaves and wood and flowers and grass and vegetation, there were instead, the odours of powder and perfume and tobacco and sweat and gin. But like the scents of the woodland it all seemed to meld into one. But where the smell of the forest becomes fresh and warm and alive in its tangibility, the people exuded an overwhelming malodorous stench of which they were totally unaware.

And they stood with their outstretched necks to be the first to see the parade. With the elders telling of the first, early circuses. Just a few men, they would say, some dancing horses, a couple of stalls but not much else. Now though, they were promised so much more for their sophisticated regency tastes. Wild eyed horses and clowns. Acrobats and singers. Boxers and giants. Dwarfs and educated dogs. Freaks and fighting cocks. Beer and skittles. And look, here they come. Prancing and dancing, the steeds with their harnesses winking and chinking in the sunshine. Tumblers rolling and turning in the dust. Musicians piping and panting with their bright instruments filled with magic.

And lissom, full-breasted maidens strode by waving pennants in the tiny breeze, filling the day with wondrous colour. And somehow, it was as if the people, the animals and all the circus folk had been carried away with the warmth of the morning, away from the real world. And for one short moment they were all being cradled in a gigantic, gentle hand suspended magically in a mystic new reality, able to laugh and cry and sing and play, cocooned, protected from the ills of life. They though, were unaware of the passing moment. Unable to recognise that that holy state of being could be theirs forever, if only they knew how. The people, in their frocks and smocks and fashionable finery.

THE HOMELESS MAN

AND he was the homeless man who slept in alleys and dined on charity. Everything he owned had originally belonged to another. Threadbare clothes snatched from a now naked scarecrow, battered shoes begged from a generous farmer, incongruous tall brown hat lifted from the head of a slumbering donkey. But it was more than that, more than the stolen, begged and borrowed things he wore, much more. Even laughter belonged to others. He could not share, for example, the joy of passing strangers. Happiness glimpsed through a warm window. A child's chuckle.

These things brought, perhaps, the stirrings of vague memories to him but did not belong to him as he shuffled over the land. Music too, was a stolen pleasure, a vicarious thrill. The singing of a church choir, the soft strumming of a harpsichord, a world and a wall away from him. A drunken fiddler in a boisterous inn, the beguiling serenade of an ardent lover. None of these were his, nothing was. Save perhaps, the grass bending beneath his tread, the green-brown veined leaves on the laden trees, the flowers exploding into colour with the riotous dawn, the call of the fox echoing through the sombre clouded night.

And he sat beneath a tree chewing a berry and watched the boxers as they bare-fisted their way to ultimate victory, ultimate defeat, to mindless insanity, and he wondered at it all. He shivered in the heat of the day. "Someone walked over my grave" he muttered. He looked over his shoulder into unseen green eyes, unaware of unspoken words that fell like stardust from the heavy laden branches. "You are not alone" they said beseechingly, "for I am always with you". But he could not hear them, the homeless man who slept in alleys and dined on charity.

THE BEREFT

AND he was the man who had looked into the unheralded eyes of death. He had stood by the rough pallet of suffering, had watched as the slender, tender fingers of the angel had prised the unwitting soul into another world. Surprisingly, it had been tender, almost loving and had left the aroma of spring's new blossoms floating, inexplicably upon the tear-laden air. And there had been a final, fleet-winged smile of recognition, a whispered word of inextinguishable love. And his heart trembled with a tide of unspoken endearments as he gazed down upon the face before him. It was as if he were attempting to record every nuance of the countenance, trying to absorb it into his being, crush it to him as a flower is pressed between the leaves of a book. To preserve it for always, to possess it and be able to look upon it in moments of precious remembrance.

And now as he stood by the white fence watching the flaunting, jaunting horses and their gaudy riders, as he observed the astonished crowd, smiling a little at their wonder. He was suddenly surprised to see the face engraved upon each of theirs. Old and young, male and female they all wore the face that he carried within his soul. He shook his head, trying to clear the vision, but without success. There it was before him, dancing, laughing. Filling the red and yellow summer morning. And he yearned to kiss it, to still the longing that lurched yet in his unhealed heart. And he wanted also, to flee from it, to bury his private grief in his own untended garden of regret.

But later, as he lay alone in the night, listening to the creaking of the darkness, the scuffling of unknown creatures, the crying of hungry birds, he discovered that the face he had seen so clearly, was gone beyond recall. Was a haze, blurred like a fish in the depths of rippled waters, like a shadow moving in the mists of morning. And he wondered, as he lay in the gloom, at his unresolved longing. Felt the unshed tears rising up in his throat and sobbed in his desolation as he attempted to bid a final farewell to the haunting shades of lost love. And blew a small kiss into the depths of midnight, the man who had looked into the unheralded eyes of death.

THE KING

THE man in green was a king, a ruler with no land, an emperor without dominion. But his palaces were everywhere, concealed within the treetops, hidden in the hedgerows, shrouded amid the rushes that swayed beside the gurgling brooks. And his courtiers were the great and small. The mighty eagle and the bright-breasted robin. The dawdling snail and the fleet-footed hare. The humble bee and the lumbering cow.

And these were the creatures with whom he shared his Kingdom, gladly, and with a light heart, for they knew him. Were aware of his presence as he walked invisibly among them. And they sang and soared for him. Buzzed and bellowed and cried and crooned for him as he kept a part of the land sacrosanct for them. And touched them with his being, preserved their innocence, and reserved a place for them in his holy hollow. And watched in despair as humanity rampaged through the world, destroying and desecrating with blind, self-righteous malice.

THE POET

AND he was the poet who wove his web of words, tall and dark, with brown hair that fell like a wing of an eagle across his lined forehead. Slender, almost emaciated he was. Standing there as if the faint breeze would bear him off in its gentle arms. And his eyes were scurrying to and fro, deep and thoughtful, watching, wondering as he composed his rich verses. Simplicity was his watchword as he attempted to paint his thoughts and dreams onto the page. But more than that, he wanted, needed his poetry to enter the soul of the reader, the listener, to be able to live in harmony with that which dwelt therein. "Everyone should be able to understand" he said, "poems should not be the exclusive preserve of the educated and erudite".

As a youth he had read and abandoned the incomprehensible convoluted writings of his contemporaries, penned as they were, for the select few who possessed the sophistication to pretend, in most cases, that they understood. No, he thought, I want my poetry to be different, I want it to reach out and touch everyone, to move them, to make them laugh, cry, feel. It should become a part of them. And he wrote of sunsets aglow like burning red fires against the gaunt treetops. He wrote of shipwrecks and lost lover's white bones washed by mystic waters at the ocean bed. He wrote of night on the open empty road filled with strange sounds and hidden perils. And he wrote about buxom, full skirted maids who frolicked bare breasted, ripe in the ripening corn. Cavorting fiery cheeked amid the splendour of summer. Lying sensuously with spread legs and white thighs and throaty laughter in deserted barns filled with naught but fulfilled promises. "Rude and crude?" he answered his critics, "perhaps it is, but they can recognise it, they can know it. It is them".

And he wondered the land, meandering from town to growing town, filling them with his words. Leaving a small legacy of himself in the minds of the townspeople who had heard him in the tavern, in the square, in the bookshop. And though he was unaware of it, his rhymes would become a part of their folklore. Would, in far off years, be set to simple music by unborn singers to set the world a ringing. And much later, in a time and a world undreamt of, beyond the imagination of the poet. In a night when the moon rides high in a blameless sky, when the wine glistens red in a flawless glass, when the logs burn and sparkle in an ancient hearth, and lovers lie dreaming on a white carpet his words will still echo on the air.

But that is for his unknown tomorrow. Now is all that concerns the poet. This day, this circus, these people, the animals, the excitement, the smell, the noise. This was all he cared about, and he opened his eyes, stretched his imagination and painted his vision of matchless rhyme upon the canvasses of time.

And he was the poet who wove his web of words.

THE LOVELESS MAN

AND he was the loveless man who smiled and cursed his frustrated desires. He stood smartly by the roadside in his tight, light breeches and shiny boots. With his fashionable cutaway coat of crimson and ruffled silk shirt, his soft tawny hair hung low and unpowdered over his upstanding collar and his honest brown eyes wandered idly over the colourful crowd as they surged along the dusty path to the circus in the burgeoning warmth of the day.

And he wondered as he surveyed them, couples, families, groups of gossiping youths, at his own burning solitude, at the unquenchable ache that throbbed deep within him. He watched the young maidens walking like brilliant, glistening stars, living playthings with their bright hats and multicoloured parasols. Smiling eyes filled with mystery. Tightly bodiced, bright hued gowns, dainty feet tripping along in sequined shoes, hands a flutter in half suppressed merriment. And he watched in envy, the swains that strode confidently beside them, chattering like squirrels, flattering like lovers. Eliciting arch smiles and arched eyebrows from them in response to their risqué little jokes.

And he wanted them all, the girls, wanted the warmth of them, wanted the touch of them. Needed to feel the softness of silken arms about his neck, of satin lips burning into his own, needed their love, their understanding. Softly whispered endearments in the afterglow of spent passion, fingertips like butterflies brushing tears from his grateful weeping eyes. And there was a pain deep within his body, a lurching, tearing, serrated knife that sliced through his loins, a bubbling churning red mist that filled his head, that obscured the day as he leaned his back against a tree for comfort till the throbbing had passed.

And then he saw her. A young girl gliding delicately along the path. She wore a gown of blue and gilded yellow and her hair was long, red like coral reflecting the light of the sunflooded sea. And her eyes were the blue of new spring filled with the joy of birth and her lips were the lips of love. He smiled at her, astonished at the perfection of her white breasts as they almost spilled from the top of her lace edged gown, bowed with his hat in his hand. Would she, he hoped heart in mouth, be the one who would take him, hold him, love him and ease the anguish that flowed unchecked through the desolation of his veins.

She looked at him, and for the briefest of moments the day stood still, but she shuddered perceptibly and walked on. Did she hear the sob, he wondered, that escaped from him as he watched her hurry away along the sun-baked path? Perhaps, but she made no sign of acknowledgement. He replaced his hat, allowing his fingers to dwell for a moment upon the great purple disfigurement that marred his face. His fingers pulsed there as if wanting to tear the mark from him, to fling it into the dust, to stamp it out like an abandoned memory. But instead, he shrugged and watched, and waited for the next girl to hove into view. The loveless man who smiled and cursed his frustrated desire.

THE DANCER

AND she was the dancer with her silver shod feet of mercury. And she kicked and cavorted and waltzed and whirled. With her soft brown arms waving and stretching. With her long black hair tumbling. With her eyes a gleam and her lips aflame. She skipped and turned in her full skirt of black taffeta and blouse of embroidered white to the sound of pipe and drum and fiddle.

She entranced the onlookers with her eldritch skills, dancing faster, and yet faster till the people grew dizzy with her gypsy movement. As she whirled they could see beads of perspiration agleam like dewdrops upon her forehead, could see the frantic beating of her heart as it heaved in her breast. And they were fearful for her, that the strain would prove too great for her fragile form, and though they wanted her to continue the dance, there was yet, a part of them that hoped she would stop, would rest awhile. That the red flush in her cheeks would subside and she would be like them, normal.

But she could not relax, for it was her very abnormality that attracted them, that made her so special for them. And so she danced on, her mind a blank, save for the next step, the next tune, and the final, frantic burst of applause that hung on the air with the dying, fading music. She could relax then. Could sit in the long grass with a flagon of cool cider, with a hunk of fresh baked, sweet smelling bread. Could gaze smiling up at the birds. Could watch them wheeling and turning in the skies as they performed their own magical winged ballet in the treetops. And who would be there to applaud the birds when their singing was over, when the night fell and their dance done? The woodlands would be empty then, for nobody ever noticed the birds, so natural was their talent.

And it was the same for the Romany dancer. She knew that if they saw her often enough, she too would become commonplace, a bore. And so she created new steps, fresh choreography, different terpsichorean feats to amuse the crowd. Burning her young body out in the heat of the day, head pounding, legs aching, blood coursing. And she wished she could be a bird, soaring in the sky with them, filled with effortless joy and colour. Blessed with the ability to fill the world with the fruit of unsurprising art. And she lay upon her back with her skirts high allowing the tender zephyrs to wash across her aching legs and breathed deeply the scents of the day. The dancer with her silver shod feet of mercury.

THE HORSEMAN

AND he was Jack Carter, the horseman with his tricorn hat, his hose and bemedalled tunic. He sat majestically upon his dappled stallion and peered at the audience, enjoying the expressions of expectation on the sea of faces. He smiled at them and persuaded his steed around the ring waving his velvet hat in the still air. This was the part he loved the most, to feel the warmth of the crowd. To be able, almost, to touch the exhilaration that emanated from them. To be inspired by them to ever more daring feats of equestrianism. Heart stopping perils that had the crowd gasping, calling for encores.

And he often dreamed of the long journey he had made to the circus, not this day, but from his very beginnings. From the time when he had been a child, apprenticed to a chair bodger. Walking the wild woods in search of fallen branches, gathering them into his rough barrow, to trudge back and turn them, fashion them into crude furniture. Small items that would, in turn, be hawked around the inns and taverns of nearby towns. But much as he liked the feel of the wood, rough in his hands, the smell of it, the malleability of it, he was bored. He was unable to visualise himself growing old surrounded by sawdust and chippings. No, he needed something else, something to stimulate him, something to set the blood acoursing through his veins, but he knew not what.

But he used to see the horses wandering through the trees, used to watch them munching the foliage that grew unchecked throughout the forest. Ah, that was better. And he loved the horses, would find the time to talk to them, croon to them, stroke them, feel the mighty muscles that rippled beneath his caressing fingers. And he would breathe his scent into their nostrils that they would recognise him thereafter, would trust him, would allow his weight upon their unbroken backs as they trotted through the bright and shaded woodland.

Then one day, selling chairs in the marketplace with the merchants, he saw the soldiers come, saw them in their bright red coats astride their steeds, with swords and muskets glinting in the sun. Saw them and suddenly accepted the shilling, drank the flagon and ran off with them. No more the woods of Wycombe for him. Now he would ride the warrior's mount. Now he would fight and kill across the ravaged war weary fields of Europe. Now he would be found telling tales of battle beneath the stars. Wiping the blood of the foe from his steel beside the flickering firelight. No more the humble woodgatherer, now he was a hero, impetuously hurling himself into unequal conflict against the timorous enemy. Steering his horse, amid the sounds of cannon and rifle and dying men, into untold danger.

Till after ten heady years he retired with his stripes and medals and honours, and the gift of a horse of purest white from a grateful colonel. And returned scarred and unemployed to the land of his birth. And took his horse and trained it, loved it, cared for it. And went awandering from town to town, fair to fair leaping and turning and balancing upon its broad back for the edification of the populace. And he purchased more horses, learned to ride them two and three at a time. Performing his fearless summersets from one to another, laughing at the oohs and aahs that greeted his expertise.

THE MAN IN GREEN

And now half a decade later he celebrated his thirty first birthday by parading his own circus through the town. It was his troupe that erected the bright tents and white fences and performed beneath the clear blue sky. His name on the gaudy posters, and he was Jack Carter, the horseman with his tricorn hat, his hose and bemedalled tunic.

THE DREAM

THE man in green is a dream. And deep in the heart of the never ending night, he is the light that dances just beyond the reach of faltering, outstretched fingers. It is he who hovers there, flickering brightly against the blackness of the sky. And he is called hope. And he is the manifestation of the inexpressible desires of mankind. And he is tantalising in his nearness, but somehow, just as the dreamer approaches on tentative feet, the light recedes, vanishes, and the enlightenment contained within subsides, to become concealed in the depths of the ebony darkness.

The man in green is the unknown dream of humanity, and sometimes there are special moments. Treasured slumbering times when the jewels of him can be felt. Warm microseconds when the soul of the sleeper can be comforted by the flames of him, can absorb the heat and the knowing of him. And suddenly the dreamer becomes omnipotent, almost at one with the growing greenness of the essence of him. But just as suddenly, in the twinkling of an opening eye, the comprehension of him is dissipated with the brightness of a new day. And the awakened one is left with a dream beyond recall, a faint unknown melody singing soft in the air, a touch of denied immortality, the frustration of nearly, nearly knowing everything.

THE CLOWN

AND he was the clown with his gin bottle, his back to front hat and his white painted face. Mr Merryfellow, they called him. And he staggered as if intoxicated in his baggy coat and too tight pantaloons. He caused the crowd great jocularity as he careered around the ring getting in everyone's path. And the horses ran into him, knocking him head over heels in every direction. The jugglers too, were made to drop their clubs as he shambled, bottle in his mouth, in front of them. And the projectiles struck him on his head, his shoulder, his arms as they fell to the ground.

And the audience laughed, whistled and hooted their appreciation of his antics. But Mr Merryfellow was totally unaware of their plaudits, as he weaved his unsteady way around the enclosure deep in conversation with a crimson coated monkey perched upon his free arm. "Ah yes good sir", he said to his simian companion, "I am truly a learned man of surpassing intellect". And he paused for a moment, head on side, nodding, as if listening to a whispered reply. "Shakespeare, of course I am acquainted with the great bard, why I had tea with him just the other day". And thus saying, he posed theatrically in the centre of the ring and drew a sword from his belt. "Is this a dagger which I see before me?" He quoted grandly. "No" roared the ringmaster, "it is a horse and rider". And the crowd roared again, as somehow the weapon became entangled with the saddle and tipped the poor rider to the ground where he lay groaning and moaning in feigned agony.

"Oh woe, woe", the ringmaster cried, "who shall now ride this fine steed for the pleasure of the people?" And there was a hushed silence before Mr Merryfellow passed the monkey into the care of the injured horseman. "Fear not good master", he said, taking a deep draught from his bottle, "for I will undertake to mount the animal if there is no other candidate". And he climbed upon the horse, back to front, placed the empty bottle upon the saddle and proceeded to perform a headstand on the fragile vessel, guiding the animal around the ring with his feet waving in the air and his arms gesticulating frantically as he went. The crowd were astonished and clapped and stamped their feet in appreciation.

After several circuits Mr Merryfellow leapt to the ground, whipped off his hat, wiped the paint from his face to reveal himself as Jack Carter the circus owner, which brought forth even more tumultuous applause. He bowed to them and left the ring, and he knew that they all loved him for his equestrian skills, but suspected that they loved him the more as the clown with his gin bottle, his back to front hat and his white painted face.

THE PUGILIST

AND he was the pugilist with his broken nose and melting brain. And he lived in a world of blood and sweat and pain. And he stood and swayed trying to watch his opponents through a crimson haze of bitter tears. His fists of clenched iron would flail around attempting to connect with unseen targets, but more often they would merely swing wildly in the overheated air.

And he inhabited an arena of agony for coppers. But it was not always so. Once long ago, he had been lauded, feted as the bare knuckle champion of all England. And money and prizes had come his way in abundance. Wine and women had been sweet upon his lips. Friends flooded to his side with honeyed words as victim after victim had fallen foul of his powerful punches. And he dodged and ducked and laughed his way through life with another adversary always awaiting his fate. But there was always going to be one contest too many, always that one lucky punch to set the stars advancing behind his eyes, the bells aringing in his ears.

And gradually the reflexes grew sluggish, the pain became a constant unwelcome companion, and those who had once made fortunes on his success, now placed their wagers on his antagonist. And slowly, slowly the friends disappeared, the wine stopped flowing and only the whores, the harlots were there to comfort him in the pain filled aftermaths of his defeats. But he continued to fight, blood pouring like a fountain from his weakened eyes, from his nose, from his torn and toothless mouth. And where once he had heard the sound of praise and applause, there was now strangely, only the sounds of the sea. The echo of the tides rushing angrily over the battered rocks washing upon the sands of his doom.

And he could feel his heart pounding fit to burst. And he was so tired. Weary enough to sleep on his feet. Sleep forever, swaddled in the paradoxical comfort of his all enveloping anguish.

And he was the pugilist with his broken nose and melting brain.

THE RAINMAKER

THE Man in Green was the rainmaker. It was he, who in the youthful brightness of the early spring, caused the rains to fall, to wash the earth, to feed his beloved trees. And it was he, who in the heavy heat of still summer, filled the sky with ominous black clouds, to empty them upon the dry, cracked and parched fields. And it was he, who in the deepness of the late dying autumn, emptied the clouds in the winds of the forlorn night spilling the droplets upon the leafless trees. And the traveller on the highway hurried along his lonesome path, feeling the rain on his lips, wondering why it bore the acrid taste of bitter tears.

THE BLACKAMOOR

AND he was the blackamoor, clad in golden breeches and white hose. He pursued his mistress to the circus, trotting in her elegant wake with a jewel the colour of flame sparkling in his blue turban. And he bore with him, clutched in his small hand, a silver sequined receptacle which contained his lady's perfume, her smelling salts, some coins, a handkerchief and an exquisitely embroidered fan from China. These items he would carry with him against her needs, and would proffer them as required.

And he was adored by all who gazed upon his shining ten year old countenance. And he, in his innocence, returned the love bestowed upon him. He danced, he sang, and he laughed, mouth wide with wondrous white teeth agleam against the pure black of his complexion. And his great brown eyes were alive with excitement as he followed his lady in the heat of the day. With the mighty sunfilled sky stirring the embers of hidden, forgotten memories of another place, another time. Of a land far away, shrouded in so many mysteries he almost believed it to be a dream. But it was a dream of surprising clarity, in which he saw himself run naked to the crystal stream which flowed beneath alien trees. In which he leaped and played in the cool water which meandered down from the white capped mountains.

And he dreamed of spears and shields. Of the roar of exotic creatures concealed in the depths of endless forests. And in his dream he was always a child. A child who dreamed

THE MAN IN GREEN

of fear. And knew not why. For here he was another child, clad in richness as he shadowed his mistress to the circus. And she wanted him to remain so, an infant suspended perpetually in time. But the years will roll, and the child would become a man, and with that maturity would come a man's desires. And a river of woe and tears and pain would flow without reason or need from his ripened loins. And nobody would ever understand why.

And he was the blackamoor, clad in golden breeches and white hose.

THE FREAKS

AND they were the freaks standing in their booths of voluntary degradation. There was the giant, seven foot six he was, but the sign said –

"At nine foot four, he is the tallest man in the world".

And in his mighty brown boots atop his pedestal, so he appeared as he looked down at the open mouthed stream of people as they passed him by. And he watched them in return, dreaming of being normal, to have ordinary hands, supple and slender rather than the massive limbs that he rested upon his hips. To have fingers that could caress a woman, could wander like butterflies across a pliant body, to be able to take a maid in love, tenderly. To be able to find a willing partner, rather than the occasional drunken whore whose fears would be stilled by gin instead of his honeyed words of sweet seduction. And he stood there listening to the gasps of amazement that emanated from people who spoke of him as if he was unable to hear. They mocked him, laughed at him, and the children were afraid of him. And his vast chest heaved convulsively with great sigh filled with unshed tears.

The bearded woman too, came in for her own share of derision as she sat elegantly upon her fine chair. She wore a gown of purple, and as she crossed a graceful leg they could see her ankles and dainty feet in silver slippers. And they could see her soft breast rising and falling, straining against the fabric of her bodice. And they stared boldly, trying to reconcile the trim, shapely figure with the hirsute mass that grew unchecked from her face. And she, in silent answer, stared back as if daring them to comment on her oddity. And there was a small smile a playing around her red painted lips. If only they knew. If only they knew that her name was not Thomasina, as the placard proclaimed, but just plain Tom. That it was all a sham. That the woman before them was, in fact a man. One who concealed his masculinity behind the garb of a maid, but at the same time was hiding his femininity in an acceptable charade, behind the beard of a man.

The fat woman and the human skeleton shared a booth, as later they would share a bed. Hiding from prying eyes beneath a coarse blanket as they proved to themselves, no matter what the crowds thought earlier, they were really no different from any of them.

And there were midgets there, running and tumbling. And a holy man from the Far East who lay upon a bed of nails and skewered himself on meat hooks. And a five-legged dog. And a rabbit with teeth half a foot long. And a man who ate fire. And a horse that could count to ten with a nod of his noble head. And the onlookers applauded wildly as they enjoyed natures aberrations spread out like some misbegotten tableau before them.

Later though, as they headed for home on their normal legs, to their commonplace lives, did they perhaps feel a touch of guilt, a twinge of pity for the freaks in their booths of voluntary degradation.

THE WANDERER

AND she was the wanderer walking through the summer flowers. In her bright bonnet, with her shining eyes she strolled across the multihued fields plucking blooms of red and blue and brilliant yellow as she went. And from her lips came the gentle sound of an unwritten lullaby, that she sang in reply to the voices of the birds who swooped and soared in the clear air overhead.

And the day was filled with an almost overwhelming aroma of ripe flowers, of dewclad grass, of mature corn, the smell of growth. And in her ears, like a distant dream, she could hear the far off sounds of the circus being wafted to her. Faint cries. Sudden laughter. The echo of drums and fife and flute, the whinny of a startled steed, the sound of bells. And she smiled for the naïve manufactured pleasure in the ancient meadow and looked upon the reality of life that coursed about her. Thistles and nettle and dock leaves in abundance. Budding elders and nestling shrubs. Bees and wasps and frantic ants. Oak and elm and beech and apple trees crowded her world. And high above a falcon wheeled and turned menacingly on the current of the air.

And there was the constant buzzing and clicking and whirring and rustling, which filled her with a joy beyond bearing, as she wandered down the well trodden path to her ivy bedecked cottage. Once there, she will take the plucked flowers and leaves, crush them with pestle and mortar to make perfumes, medicines, unguents and ointments. Bottles and jars of which lined the shelves of the candle lit room. Then, later still, she will sit by her window to watch the golden setting sun create its magical wonder upon the canvas of the sky. And count the stars as they appear like small fires in the darkling heavens. And sit at her table with a glass of plum wine, blushing red and twinkling in the flickering candle light.

And dream of her two long dead husbands. One a farmer, round and ruddy. The other a sailor lost in a storm off Biscay Bay. And she felt her body shudder a little at her memories of them. Recollections of their love. Rough love, drunken love, tender love, she had experienced it all, was thankful for it. And she dreamed too, of seven children. Some dead, some scattered like leaves in the wind. And she smiled at the memory of them over the feeling of loss and thought of tomorrow with confidence, with hope. And uttered a tiny prayer of thanks to the hidden man in the trees. The being with no name who had touched her with the essence of himself as she went through her days. Had bestowed upon her the twin gifts of contentment and humility. And she believed in him. And in return her fading life overflowed with wonder. And she was the wanderer walking through the summer flowers.

THE MAN IN GREEN

AND he was the Man in Green who stood quietly to watch the mellow middle aged world. Now it was still night, silent save for the hooting of the barn owls. For the sounds of batwings aflapping in the trees, scuffling creatures in the secret undergrowth and the sighs from his lonely heart. They had all gone now. Vanished with their prizes and presents. Weary faces, tearstained faces had all trudged off home, back along that same dusty, long shadowed path to the village, to the farms, to the taverns and to the grand mansions. And he missed their presence, hungered for the nearness of them.

The circus folk too, had packed away their gaudy tents, their exotic clothes and sat upon their wagons and rambled off into the deepening night. And he watched them out of sight, wondering how long it would be till they returned again to the ancient fields alongside his timeless woodland. Forlorn and forsaken, he wished that he too, could just drift away in the night. Could float off on the mists of evening. Be wafted way, way up into the diamond studded sky. To be able to coast without purpose or responsibility with the shades of other abandoned divinities. To meander on the breezes of time, to reach the outer limits and beyond, to become as one with the Prime Mover of all. To be happy, to be free.

And he contemplated the memory of the day, considered the people as they had passed before his unseen gaze. They were almost totally unaware of their own purpose for being, ignorant of their capacity for life. And they loved and lied, dreamed and died. Promised and perverted in their blind and blundering way through the innocent world. But although they had deserted him, renounced his knowledge, forgotten him in the chaos of their insane existence. There was yet, a small part of the mind of humanity that still, subconsciously needed him. That sought him in the hollow hours when the winds howled chill and inexplicable noises filled their souls with unknown longings.

And it was that small, infinitesimal guttering flame that tied him to them. One day, he said, one day. And he sighed again, his escaping breath shaking the leaves on his beloved trees as he moved invisibly into the heart of them.

And he was the Man in Green, who stood quietly to watch the mellow middle aged world.

THE MAN IN GREEN

PART THREE

ECHOES OF THE FAIR

ECHOES OF THE FAIR

MOST of the trees are gone now, vanished beneath the woodman's axe. Where once they stood in their hundreds, proudly, with their branches reaching out as if to touch the clouds, they stand now, huddled together, fearful of yet more depredation. The Elm had perished, dying between the sharp teeth of the voracious alien. And the Oak, of blessed memory, is left to grow in almost solitary splendour. The Beech, the Sycamore, the Walnut, they grow in less profusion now. Generation upon generation of them have shed their leaves to feed the soil, and their branches have been the homes of creation. But it was not enough, for as the trees fed the earth in their generations, so the generations of men fed greedily upon the trees. They built ships and houses and wagons and barns and fences. Sometimes they just destroyed the trees for the space created by their absence.

Gradually the shape of the land changed, where once there had been colour and life there were now only blind roads and soul-less concrete towers. And the shades of the creatures that dwelt within that vanished arborescence are weeping in the long night.

And where shall the man in green lay his ancient head?

THE MAN IN GREEN

AND he was the man in green who endured the proliferation of man. He watched them still, and wept at their frantic fecundity. They had spread inexorably across the face of the land, despoiling as they went. Unable to live in peace and harmony with their co-inhabitors of the planet, they merely laughed and destroyed, speaking honeyed words of sweet reason. Words like 'expedience' or 'survival' or 'cull'. And they spoke of conservation while breeding creatures for slaughter, wrapping their words in a package of ambivalence so that the conscience of humanity could remain untroubled.

But, the man in green mused, when all is said and done, the indifference of man always leaves a dead creature, an uprooted tree, a devastated countryside in his wavering path as he misinterprets the reason for his existence. The world, he thought, is like a fallen apple that is being consumed slowly by the very beings that need it most for their survival. For what shall remain for the children of their children when the world is left to wander empty and alone through the friendless corridors of the boundless universe.

And yet, there still remains a spark, a tarnished remnant of that which they were taught when the world was still young. It is written in faded letters upon the mouldering memory of mankind, and sometimes when the moon shines down from a clear frosty sky, it can still be seen. And it tells of music and song, it tells of art and love, it tells of benevolence and tolerance, but above all it tells of humility and justice.

THE MAN IN GREEN

And the man in green fed upon the spark, in the sure knowledge that one day it would burst again into flame engulfing the world in glory. And he watched and waited as his children flagellated themselves in frenzied futility. For he knew that mankind could not be coerced into reason, they would never come to him through fear or force. They would come to him through weariness, through hope. And they would come once more to his ancient clearing in the woods, with love, rapture, and a plea for forgiveness. And he watched and waited and remembered everything.

The man in green who endured the proliferation of man.

THE PEOPLE

AND they were the people with their bright smiles and empty eyes. They had come from far and wide to visit the show, and the sun shone warmly down on their heads as they went from exhibit to exhibit that were spread in serried ranks across the vast tree-less field. Great marquees and open trucks overflowing with all manner of goods, assailed their senses. Voices filled the air, as the vendors, anxious to dispose of their wares, cried out to the passers-by. And they were selling fruit, vegetables, clothes, craftwork, insurance, houses, membership of motoring organisations, furniture, food and alcohol. And the children with their mouths filled with ice-cream and their hearts desiring to be elsewhere followed behind their parents, screaming their indifference.

And beyond the stalls was the showground where sweating horses leapt ever higher over painted obstacles to the glory of their red-jacketed riders. And the onlookers cheered at the wild-eyed animals as the silken tones of the commentator filled the arena with false familiarity. And beyond that again, relegated to the outskirts of the field, were the naturally malodorous cattle enclosures. They were filled with animals and auctioneers, and farmers who knew what they were doing, who had always known, and who were in fact the reason for the show in the first place.

For over a thousand years the show had been held on this same day, every year come rain come shine, but where once there had been perhaps five hundred visitors buying and selling

THE MAN IN GREEN

and laughing and loving for the joy of the occasion, there were now tens of thousands of them, and most did not know what they were doing as they walked uncomprehendingly in the shadows of their forebears, trying to assimilate yet one more empty experience with which to regale their disinterested colleagues on the morrow.

And still they walked over the gasping grass, flattening it from a rich green to a pale brown, and they left the evidence of their presence upon the ground in the shape of discarded plastic cups and empty cigarette packets. Screwed up tickets and half read newspapers littered the meadow and the few remaining trees groaned under the weight of dozens of pointing placards. And they laughed and listened to the raucous music that poured from the overloud and overloaded speakers.

And the day wore on, the sun in the sky was a burning ball of flame as it shone down on the multitude. And they cursed and perspired and filled the air with unspoken anxieties. And the tension hung round the field. It was a fear for tomorrow, a regret for yesterday, and a hollow gnawing vacuum for the day of the county show. And the man in green recorded it all, as he had recorded every previous show within the fathomless caverns of his all-embracing being.

And he watched them all, the people with their bright smiles and empty eyes.

THE LIMPING MAN

AND he was the man with his wounds from the war. And every year he came to the show, taking up his post in a little wooden hut in a field that was set apart from the rest. He would take a dark peaked cap from a small shelf hidden within the confines of his cabin, and, placing it upon his head he would sit quietly upon a rickety stool to await the coming of the motor cars. For he knew that his was probably the most important job of the day, after all, he thought, what chaos there would be without him to control the wilful wheeled monsters.

And he tried to park them all so neatly. He would stare at the drivers from over his bristling grey moustache, as if daring them to pass him without payment. Then he would attempt to encourage them to park in some semblance of order. He rather liked trying to get all the red cars in one line, all the blue ones in another, the greens and beiges and greys would all take their assigned places at his behest, and he would become quite aggravated when a car would appear with two or more colours on its bodywork, for it ruined the design for the day.

And he would limp after the vehicles to make them park in a straight line, and if possible, equidistant from its neighbours. Last year he had attempted to get the poor motorists to park in alphabetical order, which proved pure mayhem, for at that time of the year the owners were so busy acquiring the status symbol of a fresh car, that they could hardly recall whether they were suffixed by a 'Y' or prefixed by an 'A', 'B' or 'C'.

THE MAN IN GREEN

And they cursed him for his pedantry, that he, a non-driver, should so assail them with his will.

And even now he had a plan for the following year. He would park them in the order of their manufacture, he would have them segregated under the headings of 'Ford', 'Jaguar', 'B.L.', and there would be a special area set aside for French and American cars. But there, over in the far corner of his field was a special low-lying marshy spot that he had singled out for German and Japanese vehicles which he held personally responsible for his war wounds, and he smiled as he thought how he would park them and then pray for rain. But for the moment he continued his task until all the cars stood in their ranks, neat as a new pin. Then he returned to his little hut and took out his luncheon box filled with cheese and pickle sandwiches which he had prepared at first light, and having switched on his radio, proceeded to munch away at them while surveying his handiwork.

And the sun burned down on him as he wiped the crumbs from his moustache and he felt contentment at a job well done, and the music played softly in the background. And a gentle soprano sang 'Vissi d'Arte – Vissi d'Armoure' and he smiled, his eyes filling with gentle tears. "I live for art and love", sang the woman, and he recalled a time, forty – no, fifty years ago when he too had lived for those things. When he and the companion of his youth had lived their lives so intertwined that it was barely possible to separate them.

For five heady years between the ages of fifteen and twenty they had grown from adolescents to adulterers, they had sung together and sinned together. They had tested the waters of life clinging one to another, that each should be a lifebuoy that they should not swim out beyond their depths. And they shared their books and knowledge, exploring poetry and philosophy. And they shared their wine and their women, discovering sensation and satisfaction. Each was the half of the one coin, apart but yet, inseparable. And their friendship was an end unto itself, existing for its own sake. And they asked naught from each other save the acceptance of that friendship. That it should survive the parting of their ways. That each should take the small gifts or keepsakes of that companionship and hold on to them, that it should endure. That perhaps one day, their paths should cross again, and then, who knows?

And to that end the man sat on his stool, and watched the faces, and listened to the music, and remembered the days gone by. Heady, halcyon days. And recalled the song they had sung all those long years ago when life was filled with promise and they were both immortal. "Life has naught to offer sweeter than its youth. Golden days, golden days". And as he saw one more car stop before his barrier, he thought, "perhaps this is him". And he stood and limped towards it. The man with his wounds from the war.

THE POLITICIAN

AND she was the politician whose days were filled with confidence and whose nights were filled with doubt. She had come to the show in the bright mid morn to cut the ceremonial ribbon with silver scissors. "I declare this show well and truly open", she had said with her sincere voice. And the people had clapped politely. She then went on to wish them all success and to tell them that the show was a microcosm of the nation as a whole. To which some wit had enquired whether that was a whole with a 'W' or a hole with an 'H'. And she stared at him with a sweet smile and continued, but he had seen the look that lurked behind the sparkle in her eyes, and shuddered.

And she went on about free enterprise, about the spirit of Dunkirk, about hope and freedom. The onlookers clapped dutifully as that strange mellifluous voice hypnotised their senses till they found themselves agreeing with every word she spoke. Until much later, when they really thought about it and realised that she had said nothing. By then, of course, it was too late. They had, in fact, joined her on the podium endorsing her posture, giving her their blessing. It was only in the quiet hours, as they lay in their beds, that they could really crystallise the feelings that filled their minds, but to which they were unable to give voice in the cold light of day.

And the politician walked round the show with her entourage, stopping for a chat here, a joke there. She looked at the exhibits with apparent interest, asking questions and smiling for the cameras. But it was the man behind her, who looked at his watch before smoothly ushering her on to the next stand where the same charade would be played out. Then suddenly, she was gone, leaving the crowds smiling but empty, and they shrugged off that odd puzzled feeling they had, and went on with their day.

And the politician was driven away amid waves and flowers and security. Within the space of a mile the show had been all forgotten, speed and urgency had dulled her senses, she was unable to give sufficient time to any of her tasks. And consequently she spread herself too thinly over her days, giving to the mundane the same attention she gave to the crucial, and in time, that self-possession for which she was known would become dissipated in minutiae and lost on the winds.

And she was wise enough to realise that fact, so she ran and ran. Exhausting all about her that they should not recognise the signs, and she smiled a secret smile and hoped that she would not be found out. But when she attempted to sleep on her lonely bed, she realised that she knew, all those false words echoed on her mind. All the youthful ambitions of prosperity and unity would come to naught, she could feel it slipping through her fingers like dust and she reached out into the night to grasp it to her again, but found that her hands were as empty as her promises. And she wept with frustration at the lost promise of her youth. And she wept with shame at the unintended deception. And she rose from her bed with the moon still in the sky to salve her pain in meaningless work.

For she was the politician whose days were filled with confidence and whose nights were filled with doubt.

THE SINGER

AND she was the singer with a voice of vibrant passion. The pure tones of her youth had been roughened by the excesses of her life, where once she had sang of love in an innocent virginal tone, now she chanted her songs with a sigh in her voice and a tear in her heart. There was now a harshness in her music that twisted the soul, filled it with desire, and explored the depths of it, to leave it sweating and panting like an exhausted deer trembling in the midst of the forest. And there was a sensuousness within her expression that left her audience throbbing with unfilled desire.

She would walk onto the stage in darkness, and the silent, expectant sea of faces spread out before her would break into spontaneous applause when the spotlight lit her small trim figure as she stood alone and unmoving upon the vast podium. She would be dressed, as always, in stainless white and her brown hair cascaded down about her shoulder in a sharp contrast to her gown. And she plucked at her collar, betraying her slight nervousness as she acknowledged their greeting with a soft smile. Then, when they were all still again, she nodded to the orchestra and the sound filled the theatre, the resonance of her voice hit them like a blow between the eyes and they felt the hair on the back of their necks rising in an explicable, primitive gesture that has no modern purpose, and there was a churning and turning in the pits of their stomachs.

And she cried out over the sound of the music, singing of lost love, lust, betrayal and despair. She sang of death, of the futility of joy, and she held herself with shaking hands as she turned her face toward Heaven and accused God for His negligence, that He should allow her to be used so, abused so by the men in her life. And the words struck chords in the hearts of her rapt onlookers, filling their eyes with tears and their hearts with longing. Then, suddenly it was all over, she wiped her own tears from her cheeks, offered them a small bow, and walked quietly away. Leaving them on their feet, clapping, cheering and strangely incomplete.

She had come to the show on a sudden whim. Whilst driving alone along a country lane she had been drawn to it by some strange force. It was as if she had recognised the curves of the road and the roll of the countryside. It was as if there was an invisible cord drawing her along the baked, tree-lined road. "I have been here before" she thought, with a slight shiver, but was unable to recall when. She could almost feel it in the air, just beyond her comprehension, just out of reach of the fingers of her mind, familiar yet unrecognisable. And the man in green sat beside her in the car willing her to see the reality of it. But she could not see it, her instincts were too raddled by the pace of her frantic life, and she shuddered and put the thoughts from her. But she enjoyed her day as she walked through the showground in her sunhat and sunglasses that she wore in part for protection against the burning sun and part for anonymity.

It was good to be part of the crowd again, to eat candy floss and play with the children that scampered in the area set aside for them. And she sang them small songs that she recalled from her own infancy and felt young again. Then she sat alone beneath an aged tree and surveyed the multitude

THE MAN IN GREEN

around her. And there was a stillness in the air, a closeness to God, she thought, but perhaps it was something else, another puzzle that she was yet to unravel. She often thought of God as she lived her high pressure madcap life. She had delved into the secrets of the occult, she had examined the Eastern, esoteric religions. She had looked into the hearts of Allah, Buddha, Jesus, Moses and Confucius but had failed to see that though God is given many names, He is still the same God, and humanity is tearing itself into fragments over the journey without a thought to the destination, seeking the salvation of the vessel whilst abandoning the compass.

And the singer sighed at her inadequacy and slept in the sun. It was good to sleep alone with the warmth of the day spreading over her body, and the murmur of the show becoming dim in the distance of her dreams. And she dreamt of how she tried to seek her own redemption in the arms of a thousand writhing lovers, spilling themselves into her barren womb as she abandoned her quest for God in a frenzied maelstrom of drugs, sex and alcohol.

And as she lay with her back against the tree, her life was written in the tears upon her face. Thirty seven hectic years and all she possessed was her fame and her memories. Everything else was merely the luggage of living. Suddenly, she woke with a start and felt her cheek. She shivered again, though the day was still warm, it was as if the tear mark that had run down her face had been nuzzled by some invisible creature of her imagination. And she stood, to walk away from the show unseen and unhindered, and she did not like the feeling, she needed the adoration of the crowd – it helped her to forget the emptiness. And the man in green watched her go with a sigh, supported her arm as she went on her way, with an unseen smile of encouragement. For one brief moment she had almost come to him, she was a seeker after truth, and though doomed to failure she was most precious to him. And he would remember the value of the soul of the singer with a voice of vibrant passion.

THE CHILD

AND he was the child with the voices in his head. He sat solitary, in the small sand pit provided for the young and spilled the golden grains through his hands. His blue, five-year-old eyes examined each particle as they rained down to the ground, and he smiled wistfully as he peered at his gilded fingers. He then stood silently amidst the cacophonous sounds of the other children, almost as if he were unable to hear them, but hear them he did, and he was happy to see their merriment. His brothers and sister were there with him, building castles and playing leapfrog, and they were supposed to be looking after him. He smiled again. Let them play, he thought, as he turned to walk off into the trees as if in answer to some arcane call. His little legs carried him slowly into the archaic copse and it was as if the sun beamed down, following his every step.

And perhaps it did. For he was a chosen one, a soul reborn to carry the learning of the patriarchs of midnight into the hearts of the children of the sunrise. He would not be a teacher, he would not be one of those who stood and shouted with a voice so loud that it silenced all others, he would instead be a link in that shining chain that has stretched unbroken from all our beginnings, and will continue to infinity. And that chain is a receptacle for all the knowledge of Earthkind. And clinging to it is the way to salvation. It is a chain of gentleness forged in the heart of creation, it can be ignored but it can never be broken. And the child was a link, an unknowing link, perhaps he would never know, but the influences that radiated from him would enrich mankind, and the experiences of his life would be recorded in the hidden testaments of eternity.

And voices deep within his mind would lead him from glory to glory. And in the small heart of the tree the voice of the man in green spoke to him, and there was a rejoicing in the tones, a gentle ecstasy as the voice led the child from delight to delight. And the boy laughed with wonder.

> "Come little one, come follow me,
> We will count the waves on the wintry sea,
> Then we will look in the heart of a rose,
> To find in there that a new dream grows.
> My child, my child do not hasten away
> For I wish you to see
> The bright golden day.
> And seeing the joy of the sun in the morn
> We will find again how a new dream is born.
> I will show you the dream, you must keep it alive
> For in your hands alone can it hope to survive".

And the boy clapped his hands with glee and looked to the sky with his face radiating wonder, then raced off to join his friends again. And the man in green said softly to himself,

"It is the children, the children who are the saviours".

And his invisible arms grew great as they stretched out to embrace the innocent souls that played in the saffron coloured sand. And they looked up to welcome the shining child who came laughing and skipping towards them.

And he was the child with the voices in his head.

THE SHIP

THE man in green is a ship, a golden vessel that sails the uncharted oceans of humanity. He is a laden galleon whose hold is filled with wisdom. But he is forced to set his course to strange foreign lands. And he is driven by the storms of fate. He watches a million children running naked in the sun. He hears their youthful laughter, touches their innocence. Then suddenly, he sees them as they age in the twinkling of an eye. And their laughter turns to weeping and their virgin souls to dust, and their infancy perishes in disillusion and expires in mistrust. And it is buried in a ditch by a wall of disunity to decompose in a coffin filled with broken promises and unachieved goals.

> And teardrops fall like dewdrops
> To his pillow from his eyes
> And sadness spoils his dreaming
> Painting patterns in the skies.
> He is weeping for those children
> Running naked in the sand
> And turns to steer the vessel
> To another, different land.

Tall trees stand green against the blue of the sky and bright colours fill the land, birds flying high in the clouds, and there is a smell of flowers and the distant sound of waves breaking on an unseen shore. But as he listens he hears the song of the birds change to chants of war, and the great trees shed the leaves which fall as bombs to the earth, which in turn becomes an open sewer filled with guilt. And he closes his eyes to seek some rest. But it is a fleeting peace, for closed eyes cannot obscure the evil that has stained the land with the red of the dying. Crazy night. Endless night fleeing the light beribboned heavens. And morning comes to the man in green with an explosion of birdsong and sunshine. He leaves the ship to walk through the city, to peer around through half-closed misty eyes, nothing has changed for him. And he sees a concrete jungle filled with iron trees, and wild wheeled monsters which pour poison into the day. And the rain is falling as he walks the shining wet streets upon naked feet bravely defying the rain lashing, wind thrashing, thunder crashing day.

In solitude he floats above the cobbled streets of mankind. Till he passes beyond the steaming streaming city to come to another place that is flung to soar like a catapulted stone, that hovers between up and down. Between high and low. And in that micromoment of suspension he sees amid the black and white powder clouded sky, a multitude of faceless people who are lost as they move through their lonely, monotonous lives. And he counts them as they pass, reaching out to pluck them from the abyss. But the faceless, sightless people are unable to see him as he glides before them like a promise. And they chant a sombre song as they move into the dark grey day dawning. The wordless song becomes stamped upon his mind, and he loses himself in its strange rhythms, he sways upon his cloud filled island and dances in the new sun.

He grasps at beams of bright yellow and runs through treeland, birdland with tears of joy and pain leaping in his eyes. And he sits beneath a tree through which the golden morning

THE MAN IN GREEN

sunrise gleams, but his soul journeyed far, he stood upon the highest mountains and looked out into the depths of the ebony universe, and saw reflections in the eternal endlessness moving and shifting against a panoply of half seen stars. He saw worlds being created from matter, stars dying that have lived since time began and in death will live till the time ends. Then he travelled to the edge of the universe, far beyond the realms of death, to where he could see the world being created in an explosion of inexpressible glory, a multimillion ton planet forming within a void that was not a void. For within that apparent emptiness there dwelt the shapes and the souls of all mankind, and there was written the destinies of every creature that would ever walk upon the face of the earth.

And the man in green was unable to see them as they stood in the vacuum of illimitable time, but somehow he thought to hear their unborn souls

Sighing in the winds of creation.

THE FATHER

AND he was the father with his foothold in forever. He watched his child playing beneath the trees with its face wreathed in smiles. He laughed to himself to see the joy, and his heart was filled with delight. As he watched he felt all his cares vanish, and a warmth grew within him. It is a very few short years that the child would be really his, five small years till the calls of education drag the infant from his side, till other, alien influences are brought to bear upon the growing mind of the little one.

He wanted that there should be only happiness until that day, and he tried to hide the shadows with the sounds of merriment. There will be so much time, he thought, for seriousness and grief, that he wanted the child to be able to bask forever in the joy of its early years. To look back, when all was gloom, to those golden days, filled with music and stories, filled with sunshine or snow, waves on the seashore and protection from the storms.

He tried to offer the child that which was the best of him, for when he was dead and gone, the memory of him would be held forever in the heart of the adult who was once the child, and the value of his life would be reflected in the souls of those that followed him. He wanted that his love for the child should be a gift, and he would kiss the eyes of the sleeping child at night and thank God for the gift of its life.

"I know a land wherein there dwells

THE MAN IN GREEN

>A man as old as time,
>And if you are good he will ask you in,
>And tell a fairies' rhyme.
>Then for a while you will travel far,
>Off in a land of dreams,
>And there you will stay and laugh and play,
>Amid the bright moonbeams.
>But soon the clock strikes five years old,
>And the man as old as time
>Will touch you on the shoulder
>And you hear the school bell chime".

The little one stirred, smiling in its cot, and the father gave thanks that in this world filled as it is with all manner of wilful wickedness, there should always be the promise of new life.

And he was the father with his foothold in forever.

THE FORTUNE TELLER

AND she was the fortune teller with her crystal orb and mystic ways. She called herself 'Gypsy', but in fact she was merely a suburban housewife with dark skin and a gift for prophecy. Her small tent, emblazoned with many garish colours had been donated by the Women's Institute, and the whole project was a charity in aid of a fashionable and soon forgotten disaster. The woman sat, a little self-consciously, at her table, while one of the organisers fussed around, adjusting her head scarf, fastening one of her earrings and slightly rectifying the line of her bodice to reveal her cleavage, in what she assumed to be the regulation gypsy style.

Then with a swift pat of encouragement she was gone, leaving the fortune teller alone and wondering how she had ever managed to find herself in this situation. Surely, she thought, a talent for guessing the sex of unborn children, or the ability to win nine hands out of ten at the Whist Drives are not sufficient reason. Perhaps, she recalled, it was her long forgotten gift for palmistry that had persuaded her fellow committee members to select her. She smiled a little ruefully as she thought of how, as a schoolgirls, she had solemnly taken her friends' hands in hers and read the lines.

"You are going on a long journey", she would say, enigmatically.

"Your destiny is written on your hand like a map".

"You will have five lovers and four children".

THE MAN IN GREEN

"Someone close to you will have problems with their eyes".

All of which was probably common to all humanity, most of whom only wanted to hear the good things. But she had given it up when she had seen death in a hand, and she had wept when her secret prophecy had come to fruition, perhaps she had thought then. That there is an unknown power that moves us across the chess board of life. And she decided then to leave well alone. And it was only with the greatest of difficulty that her colleagues had been able to cajole her into doing the job today.

"It will be a lark!" they said, "don't take it seriously".

Thus she sat apprehensively at her table awaiting her first consultation.

"Cross my palm with silver, good sir", she said as the man walked in and looked at her breasts straining beneath the flimsy cotton of her blouse. She smiled and charmed him with her esoteric chiromancy. Telling him what he wanted was easy, and she relaxed. And the day wore on, each successive consultation became easier until she almost came to believe that the eldritch words she recited were the truth, and not some mumbo-jumbo reincarnated from her youth. And the pile of money grew ever greater.

Then a woman walked into the tent and sat beside her, the gypsy peered into the crystal and began to speak the words. Suddenly she realised that the reflected eyes within the crystal were not hers, these eyes were green, flecked with white, they were sorcerer's eyes and they saw into her soul, they were absorbed into her being. The words she spoke were no longer hers, rather they were the words of the all-seeing eyes.

"The will of humanity is being sapped by its own cupidity,
That which was good is replaced with that which is evil.
Sanity can not be achieved through drugs and alcohol,
Though capricious sex or thievery.
The road to salvation is found through fellowship.
It is a simple road, but you cannot see it.
And your blindness will lead to your own destruction".

She looked up to find her client gone, and the crystal was empty, there was silence in the tent, and the woman wept. The man in green went into the day and knew it was not yet the time, they still feared the manifest deity. And he offered his silent penitence to the fortune teller with her crystal orb and mystic ways.

THE REUNION

AND they were the women whose lives were overflowing with devotion. The three of them sat in the refreshment tent drinking endless cups of coffee and recalling the past. They had anticipated that there would be seven of them at their quinquennial meeting at the show, but death and the ravages of time had reduced the numbers to the trio who now observed each other sitting in their flowered frocks with faces filled with lines and fondness.

Fifty years before, eleven girls, bright-eyed with the promise of youth had sworn to meet, to renew their vows of undying friendship every five years at this place where the sun always seemed to shine. And so they did, first as college graduates, with their degrees and their hope, then as young professional women or wives. They met as mothers and later they met as grandmothers.

War and need had not disturbed the endurance of their comradeship, which filled them with joy or consolation across the long years. And the organisers of the show grew to look forward to their coming at the end of each five year period, and they would lay a table for them so as better to hear their chatter and gaiety, and on the day of the reunion there would be an expectancy in the air as the regulars would peer through the crowds to watch for their arrival, and there would be smiles of relief as the first of the women would appear in her best dress with her face wreathed with delight.

ECHOES OF THE FAIR

And the stall-holders would have little bets on who would be the first to take her place at the chequered cloth covered table. There was one very old man, who had been showing pigs at the fair since his grandfather had taken him, as a child, to win his first prize at the end of the Great War. And he would tell the newcomers the story of the women as they arrived.

"That one", he said in his rich fruity voice, as he nodded his head, "she married a lord, and her, she married a drunkard, the one in red had seven children and the one in blue had none". And he reeled off their histories to his audience as they listened in enthralled silence. "Look", he pointed, "every five years that lady travels all the way from a sheep farm in New Zealand, and that one, well, she comes from Scotland". And he gestured with a smile. "See her, the little grey haired one with flowers in her hat, she's mine and has been for over forty years and I still reckon her to be the best of the bunch". And he told how as each anniversary approached, the big red circle would appear around the date on the calendar, and he knew that his wife would want her special day off, and his heart would fill with joy for her.

But on this day the three of them looked at the empty chairs, and they realised with regret that this would be the last meeting, they were all over seventy now, but they talked like the girls they once were. Their conversation was filled with,

"Do you remember -"

"Whatever happened to -"

"Those were the days -"

And they spoke of husbands and grandchildren, pensions and politics, they told of success and unfulfilled promise, they laughed about how they always meant to see the Show but

THE MAN IN GREEN

somehow never managed to, so absorbing was the conversation. And they wistfully recalled absent friends, with their almost transparent hands clasped in a quiet prayer of remembrance.

And the air of the day was alive with chatter and merriment. And their silences were filled with the echoes of the laughter of bygone days. And they parted with hugs and kisses, and with a half humorous promise to meet again in five more years, "If we are spared", they said. But they knew. And the journey home for each of them was filled with smiles and tears, and they were possessed of that overflowing exhilaration that is beyond expression.

And they would always be there, every five years the man in green would paint their shadows upon the fabric of the days, and there would be a feeling of contentment in the wind. For the women whose lives were overflowing with devotion.

THE MIRROR

THE man in green is a mirror, and his eyes stare long and hard from within the silvery depths as he examines the soul of mankind. He has looked deeply into those parts that have been concealed from the world, and he has sighed for that concealment.

For humanity has hidden from the truth for so long, until the man in green feels that the entire world is hiding, and perhaps weeping in its secret places.

But it bleeds in public

with its sores on show

and the eyes of the mirror know, and his hidden voice whispers in the ear of humanity

In you is all good,

In you is all evil.

You share the guilt of the murderer

And the suffering of the maimed.

You are the rapist and the child killer.

And you make war on the innocent.

You are the racist and the slaughterer of everyman.

And you exist for so much more.

Yet you grasp where you can the fleeting winds of joy before you become lost in the morass of universal sorrow.

And you wash yourself in dirt and wonder that you do not become clean.

THE VICAR

AND he was the vicar with his beer and his bible. He was sitting at a table in the refreshment tent, smiling and talking softly to one of his parishioners. He had been dragged into the tent protesting, but only slightly, to discuss the price of feed, the outrageous taxes, the prospects for the harvests and many other allied topics. But somehow, each time a new subject came up, so did a further foaming tankard. Eventually the vicar was able to extricate himself and make for the outside world again, staggering slightly and a trifle red in the face, he emerged blinking into the bright sunlight.

"Morning Vicar", came a voice.

He acknowledged the greeting with a hazy smile and made as if to walk away.

"Don't go Padre, I've got things to talk about, come inside for a drink".

And the good servant of God allowed himself to be dragged back into the tent, to consume one or two more pints of strong country ale. He heard the man addressing him, but scarcely understood what he was saying. He seemed to be speaking of the sanctity of marriage and the sins of society. But all the vicar could think of was the sparkling clean air outside, and every now and then he could see the day as the openings at the front of the tent was moved to allow some lucky person to leave. He sighed and forced another drink into his unwilling mouth, he tried to say 'yes' or 'no' as required, and hoped that his benefactor did not notice.

At last he was able to leave, he weaved his way through the smoke and the tables, holding on to anything that offered itself to his groping hands.

"Excuse me", he said.

"I beg your pardon", he said.

"I am so sorry, you must allow me to replace your drink".

And so on, until once more he stood again in the open air. Somehow, he thought, the world is not as still as it should be. It was turning contrary-wise to reason, when he tried to turn right, his feet went left. The sky was still, yet the ground beneath him was moving.

"Most odd", he mumbled.

"Beg pardon, Vicar", came a voice that sounded as if it was wrapped in polythene. "Oh no, it is quite all right", he slurred in the general direction of the sound.

At this reply the disembodied voice suggested that it was not "all right".

"My word", it insisted, "you are looking positively seedy, a drink is just what you need".

And he allowed himself to be ushered yet again into the alcohol-infested air of the tent.

"Perhaps just one small sherry", he said, as he went to nobody in particular.

Ninety minutes later he was seen as he escaped, on his knees, crawling underneath the loose material at the rear of the tent, and as he went there were knowing winks and laughter.

"He's a fine man, that vicar", they said, "a pity he can't stay away from the drink".

THE MAN IN GREEN

And he lay on his back in the open air watching the trees as they whirled about him, and the black and white stripes that adorned the tent seemed to merge and separate like waves upon the sea. He closed his eyes and studied the colours created by his inner sight, great shooting stars and triangles filled his mind, red and yellow and blue washing into purples and browns across the cosmic canvas of his intoxicated brain. And the sun was high, birds wheeled and sang their songs a million echoing miles away. And he slept, in the long grass with an adventurous ant crawling across his forehead.

Long years ago he had thought to change the world. Once in those golden days of youth they had all thought that, as they talked through their nights at college. They all saw the way mankind was heading, and in their own minds they had the answer. And they wrote pamphlets and essays setting out the futility of war, after all, they believed, man has been fighting for thousands of years but no good has ever come of it. The world is as divided now as it ever was. No, they thought, we shall bring it together under the one banner of God.

But it was like shouting into a hurricane, people listened but somehow the words were swept away on the winds. And their elders told them that they should compromise a little. Things, they were told, are not what they seem. It is all God's will, and He shall reveal Himself to the world in His own time. And they were told of the glory of dying in battle for the cause of right, but they had no way of knowing which was right, for did not the opposing army have its own priests blessing the bullets and the soldiers of the adversary.

So they watered down their philosophy until it was almost indistinguishable from that of their teachers, their main

ECHOES OF THE FAIR

rebellion being to wear their hair long and perhaps grow a beard. But that in its turn hindered their career prospects, so they shaved their faces and cut their flowing locks. Instead of a vocation they now had a profession, and in shiny dog collars they went to be curators of half empty churches in small forgotten villages, and they conformed. The greatest praise that could be bestowed upon them was that the villagers would say,

"He's just like one of us". "One of the fellows".

And they lived their earnest, sincere lives in peace. Advisors, comforters, friends and advocates, they were all things to all men. But at the back of their minds they sometimes wondered what they were to God.

It was twilight when the vicar awoke, the first stars were appearing in the sky, and there was a gentle breeze in the air. The fair was still, save for a few stragglers making their way homeward, most of the lights had gone out and he could see the searchlights of the cars as they sped off into memory. He was alone now, and still more than a little drunk, he staggered to his feet with an effort. He was filled with remorse as he made his uneasy way through the empty showground. "Next year", he said to himself, "I shall be a little more abstemious".

As he wandered slowly along he became aware of not only a more than slightly throbbing head, but also a bladder that was acting like a time-bomb. He felt that at any moment it was going to explode and completely ruin what was left of his self-esteem. His weary eyes searched the dim light ahead until he saw a small clump of trees, and he made his unsteady faltering way toward them. And in the hidden night the man in green watched his approach. He saw as the vicar halted for a moment before a mighty tree that rustled softly in the cool breeze, he swayed a little and narrowed his eyes to see the better, and the man in green felt that his own eyes were being met, that his own soul was being examined.

"They worshiped you once, you great green god", the vicar said, "they came to you with their sacrifices and their prayers, they used to adorn you with flowers and dance before you in the Spring. And they would sing their hymns of hope to you". And then he paused, and the trees became silent, the rustling in the leaves was stilled and the late birds ceased the chuckling singing. Then for one brief heart-stopping moment the man in green felt that the vicar was addressing him, had acknowledged his presence in the heart of the tree. He imagined that here, at long last, the old and forgotten religion would meet and merge with the new and fragmented faith. That here, perhaps, a start could be made in the rebuilding of humanity. But the vicar continued, dashing the forlorn hopes of the aged deity.

"Ah, you great old oak, what is left for you now? It is only I who has need of you and I thank you kindly for your shelter". And he went behind the tree and relieved himself in a hissing, steaming stream of golden rain. The man in green watched and laughed softly, he was talking to the tree, the old gnarled tree, and not to him. He sighed and watched as the vicar stumbled off into the night. And he smiled as he heard him singing as he want.

> "The Lord's my shepherd, I'll not want,
> He maketh me down to lie.
> In pastures green He leadeth me,

The quiet waters by".

The voice sounded so soulful on the still night air, so full of faith and trust. The man in green looked and spoke softly,

"You came so close, my friend, so close".

And he settled himself down to continue his long lonely vigil.

"One day", he whispered, "one day".

And he called out a soft, unheard farewell to the vicar with his beer and his bible.

THE TEACHER

AND she was the teacher with her crocodile of erratic euphoria. She had attempted to organise her giggling girls into some semblance of order, but there was always one who would race out of line to stare open-mouthed at some exhibit or other, and that one would be followed by the remaining dozen, and the poor teacher would be left to call them back into line with an air of exasperated harassment in her voice. She had, after all, brought them to see the show-jumping. But there was a good chance that it would be all over by the time they reached the ring. "Come on, girls", she pleaded, reminding them that one of her old pupils was performing today. But they did not hear her, or rather chose not to hear her, as they listened to the ribald comments of the double-glazing salesmen.

And the teacher watched them and wondered what she was doing in charge of all this blossoming pulchritude. Had she really spent so much time at college and university obtaining her First Class Honours degree, merely to finish up as a fifty-five year old spinster trying to control the lusts of thirteen pubescent nymphets. And she wished she could go off and smoke a surreptitious cigarette. And perhaps a small sherry would go down nicely. She sighed.

"Come away, girls", she insisted, and watched as the uniformed line reluctantly recreated itself before her imperious gaze. Then, satisfied with the effort she clapped them into activity, and smiled thinly as the line resumed its strange meandering way. Until the next distraction, that is. She could put up with the laughter, she could put up with the sniggering behind her back, she could even accept the hilarity engendered by a horse relieving itself before their astonished gaze. But what really irked her was that when they all returned to school, the girls would produce essays of remarkable erudition regarding the agricultural heritage of England, or they would describe in great detail the glories of the flowers and fruits that had been displayed, or they would exhibit an encyclopaedic knowledge of the workings of a wide variety of tractors and combine harvesters. When really, the teacher knew, they were only interested in the bulging jeans of the youthful farmworkers. And the teacher was going to have to mark them on the quality of their work, rather than on the chastity of their thoughts.

So, upon arrival at the showground, she did what she did every year. And she left the girls in charge of an elderly female official and vanished into the beer tent for what she described as a small pick-me-up, which was in fact four gins and one packet of mints to hide the evidence. But the girls always knew, and they tried to understand. But it was all too deep for them, who were on the brink of life, to comprehend the workings of the mind of her who had watched life pass her by. So all they could do was to protect 'old Miss' who was the teacher with her crocodile of erratic euphoria.

THE FIRE

EVER upward leaps the yellow flaming fire.
And it consumes the multitude of microcosmic worlds in the ebony blackness of the soot begrimed night.

The smoke soars into the clouds losing its identity in a fusion with the drifting dreaming clouds.

And the man in green is that fire, that smoke.

And he floats unknown through the sprawling world of overpopulated humanity.

The spark of his existence stretches to absorb, to interpret that which surrounds him.

And there is a desperation about him as he tries to grasp the significance of this war or that peace, and his flame flickers madly as he attempts to relate to the seething mass of creation.

THE SALESMAN

AND he was the salesman with his soft and silver tongue. He came to this annual event each year with his anonymous truck filled with oaken furniture, and with his cajoling words and persuasive manner, he contrived to separate the passing populace from as much of their hard earned money as he could.

He dressed in elegant grey, with a white handkerchief just showing in his top pocket. His cuffs were of the purest white and adorned with links of gold. And his neat, almost military tie completed his air of honesty. His dark hair was just right, slightly flecked with grey, and he appeared to be young to the youthful and mature to the middle-aged. And the elderly thought him to be a son.

Selling, he often thought, was all about appearances, not just the way one looks, but how one acts, and the tone of the voice. It is a gentle insinuation into the mind of a prospective purchaser. The salesman must be in turn friend, confidant, lover and psychologist. And each of the adopted guises must be natural, each pose should be worn with grace and ease. There should be smiles and laughter, knowledge and silence and an understanding of the needs of the client, without forgetting the needs of the employer and the demands of one's own financial situation.

But he loved his job, the furniture filled him with delight. Made from trees that were felled before he was born and lovingly carved and worked into pieces of practical art. He loved to run his hands over the wood, feeling the strength and smoothness in it, and the strange symmetry of the grain that had been brought out by the craft of the carpenter and the polisher, to stand in perpetuity as a monument to their skill. And then there was the carving on the wood, the linenfolds and the roundels, the gothic arches and the cactus flowers. Great bulbous carved legs on tables of Cromwellian proportions and gentle tapering pedestals. And there was the smell of newly polished wood, filling his nostrils like a strange primitive perfume.

And he wanted to share his delight with the people, he called to them as they passed, but most of them merely ignored him. Or they said that they were only looking, only browsing. Or they hummed a small tune of discomfort as he approached them. And he smiled philosophically, secure in the knowledge that someone was going to buy before the day was out, one in fifty, one in hundred. He shrugged, it would be sufficient. And he watched the day and the passage of people. And dreamed his dreams. All salesmen, he thought, are really something else at heart. He felt that he should have been a doctor, or perhaps a teacher. No, he was a born actor. With his charm and his ready wit, he was made for the theatre, and he often wondered why he never became a performer. Perhaps selling was the easy option, tomorrow he could become an actor, there was always tomorrow. And he spent his day talking, persuading and flirting with the women in their summer dresses. And he was content, the salesman with his soft and silver tongue.

THE GARDENER

AND he was the gardener with his rakes and his wrinkles. And he remembered the show, which with the Summer, had gone with the winds of passing time. And he watched the red gold Autumn leaves falling, hovering on the cool air as if suspended in time and space, and he listened to them as they crackled and crunched beneath his carefully guided footsteps. They had grown and thrived in the spring and summer trees, they had been baked by the sun and soaked by the rain. Until, finally on this sparkling, dew-shining day they are released to float like dying butterflies, tenderly, gently to the ground. And he gathers them together with his great brush of twigs into piles of pungent brown heaps of decaying foliage that bears the aroma of cold Autumn nights in damp forests, rain on the breeze gleaming like sunlit diamonds that hurt the eyes. And of secret love in forbidden glades.

And the gardener's day turns soon to darkening evening, the stars look down to watch the used-up leaves as they lie upon their pyre. A match scratches into bright flame and the paraffin saturated memory of summer sunshine explodes into a tower of smoking, sparkling, firelit brilliance. And the echoes of the show are gone with the fire, and the ashes of all the shows are cremated in the flames. The birds migrate with the burning leaves lighting their way like a beacon of sorrow. And Summer has gone with the fire, young lovers walk no longer beneath the leaf-laden trees of desire.

THE MAN IN GREEN

And the gardener looks at the trees, bare and gaunt with their fingers pointing to the stars. And he walks into the night, leaving them in solitude, like all of creation, to face naked and alone the biting tearing winds of the endless, relentless winter. And the man in green turns to find his shelter and his comfort wheresoever he can, and bids his farewell to the gardener with his rakes and his wrinkles.

THE MAN IN GREEN

AND he was the man in green who endured the proliferation of man. He was not born flesh and blood, he was not born of passion or of lust. He was created, rather by mankind's own desire for his existence. Humanity developed a need for a unifying deity to control the raggle-taggle wanderings of its chaotic soul. And the man in green was begotten in the mists of the primeval marshes. He was fathered by the winds of want and nurtured in the bosom of the burgeoning forests.

He dwelt in the barren deserts, and walked alone in the wilderness. And his cry was merged with that of the eagle as it flew golden against the setting of the sun. His home was in the heart of the trees and also in the depths of the rose. He swam through the waters of eternity and made his house in the snowy wastes at the top of the world. And he could still be found smiling in the tear of a child, or in the prayer of the lost sailor calling out in the storms of the mountainous oceans. He wore the green of nature and lived in the legends of history.

And he tried to understand the monster for whom he had been created. For century after long century he had searched for the reason for the strange eccentric ways of man. The being who could both propagate and abandon him at a whim. Who could sacrifice, both to him who stood for glory, and to the strange hidden dark devils, who stood for disorder and death, at one and the same time. The being who spoke words of peace and wars in a single sentence. And sometimes he

THE MAN IN GREEN

despaired of ever comprehending their purpose. Yet, as he looked now at the people as they left the show in their ones and twos, he felt their unspoken need of him, he heard the echoes of the loneliness in their hearts, the emptiness of their longing for that which was beyond their understanding. And he wanted to reach out and touch them, to reassure them that all was not lost.

And he looked at the children, born into a life of joy and oppression, of riches and poverty. They were born with innocence and purity in their hearts, created with all the hope and promise of tomorrow, but they were corrupted by misconceived ideology, they were fed guilt that flowed in their mother's milk, and they became flawed as they breathed in the lead-laden air that swirled in heavy skies. But sometimes, as the man in green became despondent at the strange world he was forced to inhabit, there would suddenly come a being who would walk upon the earth in glory. A being who would create a line that would give more than it received, would put back into creation more than it removed. And he watched them leaving in the fading radiance of the day, he remembered the child who had heard him, who had responded to him hidden in the trees, and his heart swelled with happiness, for he had seen that same child before.

Over the centuries the child had been born and reborn, quietly spinning his web of love across the years. Tilling the soil, planting the crops, refraining from evil and filling his small part of life with unselfish devotion. And the man in green felt that one day there would be a time when he and the seed of the child would join hands, and the real would merge with the unreal in the triumphant emergence of the essence of humanity.

And he was man in green who endured the proliferation of man.

THE MAN IN GREEN

PART FOUR

ASHES OF THE FAIR

THE MAN IN GREEN

AND he was the man in green who had survived the perdition of mankind. His aged eyes had watched and wept as he had waited for them to turn to him for succour. They had attempted to reach the stars, to wander into the never-ending glory of the heavens. He could have told them that their timing was wrong. That it was impossible to spread their kind of havoc through the galaxies, they were not ready, and now, perhaps would never be. They should have solved their own problems of violence, of greed, of spiritual ignorance upon their own planet before they tried to infect the untainted universe with the ills of man. Their doom was written in their deeds, but they saw it not, as with eyes bright with avarice they grasped greedily at the fabric of life, trying to wear the crown of creation when their heads should have been covered with the ashes of guilt.

And the air was filled with disease and torment, it was as if there was a self-inflicted wound festering within the bosom of humanity, and they perished in the shining gold of the sun, they died in their millions, starving in the midst of plenty, condemned by indifference. And among some there was a death wish as they raced with each other along the suicidal path of over-indulgence. They hid in corners slowly dying as they thought to enjoy themselves by desecrating the temples of their souls. And the young perished, like flowers before they had blossomed. Dying of their diseases of promiscuity and the ills of licentiousness. And the air became unfit to breathe, the

THE MAN IN GREEN

water to drink, the food to eat. And there was a madness in the wind, the much heralded, much vaunted technology was destroying them, it was as if the rains that fell like tears from heaven was infected also as it rotted the trees, and washed away the buildings.

And it was not only man that died, it was the fields and the forests that he took with him, and the landscape changed. That which had been verdant was now barren and windswept. For mankind did not realise that he shared the poisoned cup from which he drank with the whole of creation. And the dregs of that cup spilled out from the lifeless fingers of man and infected time itself as it corroded the crystal encrusted corridors of history. And everything was forgotten. As if it had been consigned to a deep lime-filled pit of oblivion. All that was good of man was buried in that pit. Music, art, literature, philosophy, and faith. But with all of that went the evil of humanity, all the killing and the greed. All the rape and the lies, all the cruelty and the blood-letting, it had all been swept away like a small hiccup in the throat of eternity. It was as if the slate had been wiped clean, and the man in green dried his eyes and looked to pick up the pieces. Perhaps, he thought, it was this for which I was created all that had gone before merely a preparation. And he sighed and looked about him.

The man in green who had survived the perdition of mankind.

THE BEACON

THE man in green was a beacon, a tower of light that filled the world, he blazed like A fire of gold. He shimmered illuminating the trees around him. The verdancy of his garments was subtly altered by the influence of the radiance becoming paler, yet somehow retaining the essence of the greenwood. Then the colour began to change, it mixed and mingled with the blue of sky, it merged with the white of the clouds, and the sun beat down turning the edges of those clouds to red, harmonising the effect until it seemed that a thousand different shades were there. Sparks appeared to fly from the small copse where the man in green stood with his arms outstretched, a vast outpouring of multicoloured diamonds, a riot of rainbows filled the air. And the copse, which was a forest, which was a wood, finally appeared to explode in a glory of kaleidoscopic diversification. The man in green had sent out his call.

And the long persuasive tendrils of colour that had emanated from his mind stretched out across the lands. They entered the souls of the people and drew them to him. They infiltrated the consciousness of man, stealing into the long barren vacuum of his imagination and giving him hope. His colours filled the intellect, and that which had been void became full, that which had been empty and purposeless now acquired a goal. And slowly, slowly they began to be drawn towards his woodland. They came first in their ones and twos, than faster, a dozen here, twenty there. And their numbers grew and grew until they became a torrent of humanity sweeping across the countryside to his ancient clearing in the trees. And the man in green felt his heart surging with joy, and all the colours of him seemed to dance and sing as they soared towards the heavens.

THE WATCHER IN THE NIGHT

AND he was the watcher, lost in the never-ending diamond studded night. He hovered over the ever-changing patterns of the universe, he saw mighty stars a million miles wide that were lonely in the vast inky blackness. He was aware of huge constellations spinning without apparent purpose, and tiny asteroids that were no more than specks of dust, fragments of sand on the shore of the velvet eternity. And he surveyed the planets that turned in the twinkling of an eye from a mass of molten energy into useless and dead carcasses. And within that breath of time he watched and wept for the creatures of those worlds as they struggled for identity and survival against the insuperable barriers of predestined destruction. And he pondered on the apparently unplanned universe and thought to play a role in the scheme of infinity.

He contemplated the choice of stardust before reaching out his hand into the depths of space. He took a small, dead world and cradled it to his full heart.

> "This world," he said, "is mine, I will shield it and guard it from all ill, I will protect it from alien evils, and I shall breathe life into it, bringing forth a people that will rise and flourish to become like gods that their fame shall spread throughout the universe, and their wisdom and goodness shall ring to the unseen edges of the cosmos"

THE MAN IN GREEN

And he sat and planned his creation, what form should it take? What manner of being should inhabit his world? And he smiled at the joy of creation. And the universe watched also, and waited to see what would become of that particle of celestial waste. And yet, far, far away, boundless light-years distant from the watcher in the night, was the prime mover of time and matter. Beyond the stellar boundaries he watched also. And he alone knew the aim and purpose of the universal scheme. It was he that directed the stars in their courses, he caused creation to become manifest upon the chess-board of the firmament, and should it be necessary for a star to die, then he brought about the demise of that star. But now he was disturbed by the thing that had unfolded upon the fringe of the fabric of his creation. "Watcher in space," he called, "what is this deed of yours that will alter eternity. Why have you done this thing" "I have committed no great wrong," answered the watcher. The prime mover became angry

> "Do not presume to be the judge of your actions. I alone know the magnitude of your crime, I alone know that the repercussions of this thing you have perpetrated will echo beyond the bounds of the outer void. Why then, have you done this?"

> "What I have done was done out of pity for the creatures of the stars. I wanted to produce a race that would survive its desires for self-destruction. And on this one dead planet I hoped to achieve

a creation that would possess the gift of eternal growth."

"Dead" echoed the prime mover, "fool, this is no dead planet, this is but a world that sleeps for a moment on the winds of time. There was a time once, when the beings who inhabited its surface attempted self-destruction, but the time was not yet right for their departure from the scene. Look now at your planet, watcher, see what you have done and try to undo your misdemeanour, and I alone know of the tears you will shed for your folly."

And the watcher in the night went from the presence of the Prime Mover and looked upon the world he had plucked from the ether and wondered how he could repair his actions. He saw mountains, high snow capped peaks that reached beyond the full clouds, he saw rivers flowing through deep valleys and carving their way to the turbulent oceans. He watched his planet in its white, storm-filled Winter and in its burning Summer. And he realised that this, indeed, was no dead world. For within the depths of the rivers he could see fish swimming and thriving, all manner of life was there, both animate and unmoving. Insects crawled in their multimillions from the valleys to the mountain tops, and animals and birds made their dwellings in caves and trees and deserts. And he saw human beings huddled together beneath the few trees, lost and alone in the nights. And he wondered at their desolation. He looked at the landscape and saw decay. Ruined buildings filled his vision and rusted ships filled the harbours and no one seemed to care. There was a fear that pervaded the air and rotted the fabric of life, the world had lost its direction and there was no-one to point the way. And the watcher in the night shuddered, replaced the world in its predestined place in the stars, and walked off into his timeless void. But his touch and his presence had created a small nightmare within the souls of humanity, a new terror to replace forgotten fears.

The man in green watched also from his trees and he wept at his impotence against alien forces, he prayed that his work of rebuilding was not to be irrevocably destroyed before it had even begun, but there was a nagging doubt echoing within his mind as he turned to insinuate his purity into the body of the detritus of man. So long, he thought, it has been so long until this moment, have I the strength to endure it for longer? And from his throne on the edge of creation, the Prime Mover gave him comfort and courage. But he too suspected that at some future time the whole process would have to begin again. And far away the watcher cowered in a small black corner and hoped to be forgotten, but the Prime Mover, the man in green, and humanity would always recall the error of the watcher, lost in the never ending diamond studded night.

THE BOY

AND he was the boy on the road from nowhere. He lay upon the barren ground, resting, his breath came in tortured spasms and his eyes were glazed with effort. He knew not from whence he came, or how long his journey had lasted, but his legs ached, and the pain in his back hurt more with each breath. His mind revolved and turned, but there was no recollection, there was only this moment. This place where he lay on the dusty remnants of a road, and some strange inexplicable force that drew him on.

And there was a dread, a fear of something without a name. And there were sounds that echoed within his head, he tried to close his ears with his hands, but the noise was still there, it could not be erased. And he listened, and heard screams, shouting, and half-hidden grey shapes that moved with blood, red upon them. And the boy was powerless to name anything he saw or heard. He rose to a crouch and looked about him, but he did not know this place.

And the emptiness of his spirit caused him to cry out in his anguish. And the loneliness was more than he could bear. He stood upright feeling the wind on his face, and turned to where the sun rose in the dawn, his mind was empty of all that was past, all that he possessed were feelings and impulses that drove him inexorably on. He walked, he ran, but every now and then he would turn and look over his shoulder to shudder at a hidden memory, and hurry on. And the day grew older with the sun filling the sky above him, and the warmth gave him nourishment, and his heart became lighter with youthful resilience. Everything was apparently new to the boy, he saw the birds flying, capturing the moment in joyous song, and he joined them in their music, he counted their colours as they swooped and dived around his head. And his unknown fears were dissipated in a haze of, in a blaze of summer.

And he felt the sweat pouring down his spine, it was as if he were flying with the birds, soaring in the sky and floating on the white clouds. He reached out a hand to grasp a swallow that came too close and held it gently in his fingers, calming its frantic struggles with a gentle cooing sound that emanated from the back of his throat, and he was puzzled that he had the ability to sooth the creature, and wondered where the learning had come from. He looked at the bird, still now, with its small eyes fastened upon the boy's face, and all the other birds were still also, the air was empty of singing.

And the boy as he looked, felt the pangs of hunger rising in him, saliva filled his mouth and trickled over his lips, he raised the bird to his face to see reflected there that self same fear he had felt earlier. And the sky seemed to howl in terror, to tremble in despair. But the boy did not eat the bird, he merely placed his mouth against the beating heart and kissed the feathers that quivered there with fear, and released the creature with a smile. It flew high into the sky showing itself to the world in surprise, then it swooped down to the boy, circling his head before flying off to join its fellows, and they all ascended to the clouds, vanishing in the mist. But the sky echoed with their song long after they were gone. And the soul of the boy was filled with the memory of it as he followed the road.

ASHES OF THE FAIR

And soon it was twilight, the world grew silent for a small moment as the creatures of the day moved aside from those of the night, and the boy knelt by a stream drinking from his cupped hands and watching the silver fish as they swam, darting and gliding over stones washed clean by the rushing water. And he dug for, and ate the roots that hid in the marshy ground. And he wondered again, how he knew that the root was not poisonous. Where had he come from? And what was the hidden terror that lurked behind him at a point between the rising and the setting of the sun?

Far into the night he pondered on the problem, as he lay upon his back with his hands behind his head looking at the stars, as if he thought the answer was to be found in the heavens. He was not even certain that he wanted the answer to come at all. Perhaps remembering the reality of the past would prove too much to bear. For if he was escaping from terror, perhaps it would be better to not know what it was, and just keep on going.

He shrugged and his eyes followed the moon as it disappeared behind a cloud. And he listened to the sounds of the night. The cry of the nightjar, the hoot of an owl. The sudden scuffle of a mole, the beating wings of the blind bat. Then he slept, dreaming, with his thumb between his lips, he felt that he was being pressed against the breasts of a great protective mother. And he smiled in his sleep, warm and safe with the earth beneath him. Then suddenly he was awake. Fingers of fear clutching him by the throat, as he heard the howl of the killer dogs as they tore their screaming prey to pieces. And he screamed himself, his voice reverberating through the night. Now he knew the basis of his fear, he rose and staggered off. Weeping and alone.

The boy on the road from nowhere.

THE GIRL

AND she was the bronze coloured girl with the instincts of the wilderness. She raced across the mist covered hills, her nostrils flared to capture the fragrance and fear that dwells within each scent that her finely tuned nerves perceive. She can almost taste the odour of the wild cat, and she becomes the cat. Slinking sensuously through the morning, then she becomes aware of the pungent aroma of the killer dog and becomes that also. She growls softly as she pads menacingly, silently upon her toes. And the growl turns into a sinister, baying wail that she is unable to sustain. It turns then into a shrill scream which fills the air, frightening the thousand birds in the sky above her, and they wheel and turn as they fly away.

And she smiles, her lips drawing back over only slightly discoloured teeth. She knows she is not the dog, she knows she is not the cat. And she walks more slowly, her naked feet gently brushing the dead red dust that carpets the ground beneath her. Suddenly on the wind there is the smell of wild mink from the river, she can hear them rustling in the reeds, and counts the sounds. And she stiffens and quickens her pace, for she is terrified of the blind unreasoning fury of the mink. There are scars on her legs from the razor-sharp teeth of mink and wounds on her soul from the furious frenzy of the attack. And she is glad she is not a mink.

She looks up again at the birds and wishes she could be one of them, and she waves her arms against the wind but cannot fly, and her voice cannot imitate their sound, nor can her skin mirror the colours of their bright plumage. But who is she if she is not a bird? And there is the acrid smell of a fox on the air, her eyes narrow and her lips curl cruelly, she lowers herself to the ground snarling as she does so, and the girl feels that she is a fox, she thinks like a fox, moves like a fox and acts like a fox as she pounces upon a slow moving rabbit which she tears to pieces with her strong fingers and sharp teeth. She consumes each part of the doomed creature and smiles as the still warm blood trickles down her half naked breasts.

Her eyes close at the ecstasy of the kill and she clenches her fists until her long nails draw blood from the palms of her own hands, and the two bloods mingle, that of the rabbit with that of the girl. But there is yet a third blood mingling, it is the blood of the fox who has become the girl as she lays down to rest in the shade of a single oak, and the mistletoe hangs heavy on the bough. Her eyelids tremble in half slumber, and she dreams of running and eating and sheltering from the storms of winter, she dreams also of returning to the fires of her home and of her family who despise her. She remembers the bull-like man who was her father, of her mother who did not see her child growing from her until it disappeared, finally becoming her rival, not her daughter.

And they gave her no name. Only her brothers had names. The girl remembered the ceremony as her father had squeezed the white juice of the mistletoe over the heads of each in their turn. He called the eldest, 'Tree', in honour of the oak for which he had no name, only awe for its prolific growth. The second son was called 'Bird', for the eagle, that great creature with its terrifying visage. The third and last son was called

'Death', for the wasting illness that was born with him. And the girl had watched, saying naught.

Now though, she dreamed and she wept in her dreaming with her mind wandering in restricted circles as it attempted to struggle from the vacuum of her ignorance. They gave me no name, she thought. And it was the name that created a person, gave substance to a life, gave dignity and purpose.

But she possessed the knowledge of the land, and that was better than nothing. And she grimaced in her sleep for she knew that knowledge of the land was all that was available to her, all else was shrouded in mystery. And her tears were tears of frustration for all that she would never know. She had seen the snows of winter melt seventeen times, she was full grown in mind and body, yet she was empty. Her dreams were like a prayer, a hoping that perhaps there was more, but more of what? And she had recollections of her journey from her hated home, broken buildings covered with weed filled the landscape, dead trees lay destroyed by time, and towns, cities, stood abandoned by all save the killer dogs and the voracious rats, grime ridden edifices filled with legend and pain. She would never enter a town, instead she left them to decay.

Then, as the sun began to sink in the heavens she opened her eyes, felt the tears upon her cheeks and a strange sadness came upon her, she felt bereft, alone and friendless in a world without pity. She looked at the bones of the eaten rabbit with remorse. She wanted to say sorry for its harsh death, but she had no word for sorry. Instead she took the bones and made a small pyramid of them, she surrounded them with dead leaves and twigs, then took two pieces of wood and rubbed them together till they became a blur, sweat poured from her with the effort, and she was impervious to the pain in her arms. Suddenly a small glow appeared, and she blew on it till it became a spark, then a series of sparks, it became a flame, then a fire, the leaves and twigs became a furnace that consumed the bones of the dead creature.

And the girl watched the flames and her eyes followed the smoke upwards till it disappeared into the heavens. Somewhere within her, then, was born the concept of freedom, albeit the freedom of death, but nevertheless, as she watched the smoke vanish, she wondered where the rabbit had gone, and was it now, perhaps, safe from its foes. She wished that she could be the same. And she walked slowly from that place, scowling, for she had no words to describe the feelings that were deep within her, and smiling for she knew that she was not really the fox.

At last it was night and she watched the mists rising from the river until everything was obscured by the swirling greyness, and she watched as the road ahead vanished before her eyes, and she fearfully hid herself away for the night thinking of her father, who used to tell tales of the fog to his sons. He would tell of strange men who moved mountains and cast curses. Men of violence who killed and wounded, creating vast earthquakes and creeping pestilence. And in the telling, she recalled, he became as terrified as his sons, and they pulled their garments about them and huddled closer to the fire.

She shuddered at the memory, but she was glad she would not see them again, her destiny, she felt, was somewhere along that empty dusty road. She sank to the ground and lay staring up at the bowl of the night, and the half-hidden stars caressed

ASHES OF THE FAIR

her eyes, wiping away her tears. The moon sailed hazily across her vision and she slept, undisturbed but every ready for instant action, for she was the bronze coloured girl with the instincts of the wilderness.

THE SEER

AND he was the seer with his dreams and fancies. He walked the land upon stunted legs, limping away across the countryside with a wooden staff clutched between the three fingers of his left hand, his good hand, he called it, for his right hand was withered completely away, ending as it did in an unsightly stump. And around the wrist of that useless limb was tied a cord which held his pack slung over his bent shoulder.

His hair and beard were long and unkempt, and a madness burned in his deep-set, constantly moving eyes, and a great pulse was throbbing away in his furrowed brow. And he carried his head to the side, as if to detect every nuance of every sound that filled his ears. But he was unable to tell whether those noises he heard were real, or were they, he wondered, merely another dream. He heard songs in a land without music, laughter in a world without joy. He heard the rumbling sounds of engines, the roar of unseen technology. And the cries of unborn souls filled his days. But were they perhaps, the sighing sobs of long-dead sacrificial lambs, he could not tell.

And therein lay his madness. He could read the landscape and wear the cloth of creation. He was aware of the desolate landscape, but saw the shadows that lurked in the long vanished hedgerows, and in a world filled with ignorance he shared their arcane knowledge. He knew of gods and legends, of stars and sciences. He knew the tragedies and triumphs of long buried souls. But yet, the things he knew were unknowable, they had no form or existence. But yet, the visions flew through his consciousness tearing his brain apart, and filling him with rage and pain. They passed through his imagination, wild incarnations whirling like the wind, manifestations of gold and shining silver dancing weirdly in the maelstrom of his despair.

He saw strange pictures of people riding the untameable shimmering blue skies on wagons of winged marble. And he watched them as they played in the sunshine, singing beneath the leaf-laden trees, and he heard their shouts of joy as they swam in the rippling white flecked water with their bodies whole and untouched by the poison that seeped from the pits of despair. Then with the ebbing sun casting its golden shadows upon them, he watched them in their fearless love. And he smiled a little wistfully at the sight.

Soon though, the passing images gathered pace, the leisurely lyrical visions faded from his view to be replaced by a million flashing pictures of light and fire. There was fear and violence and panic, the reflections that appeared before his raddled eyes came and vanished faster and faster till he could hardly comprehend that which he saw, until at last it was as if a mighty universal scream filled his senses and he clawed his head with his fingers, hiding his eyes to shut out the light.

Later, he lay upon the ground with his pack beneath his aching crown and looked up into the darkening sky. A small tear ran down his cheek as he counted the stars that appeared in his heaven, but which somehow shared the space with the illusions of another world. "I am the receptacle of all mankind",

THE MAN IN GREEN

he murmured, "and my despair is the despair of everyman. The memories I have are the memories of humanity". And he wanted to rip the top of his head to shreds, to tear it open so everything that was imprisoned there would pour from his brain, spilling out onto the barren ground. Then, he thought, it could all be revealed. It could feed the land and restore it, a million people could cavort upon the earth, released at last from his imagination. All the lovers, all the warriors, all the children, all the helpless and the homeless would cast aside their crutches and dance naked and unashamed in the moonshine.

And the cascade would continue like a multi-coloured waterfall pouring from his mutilated head, all the visions and memories of mankind would etch the landscape with glory, flowing and flowing, flowering and flowering till the torrent becomes a trickle, gently releasing at last the earliest recollection. Would it, he thought, be a memory of his birth, his conception. Or perhaps a memory of the birth of man. Or even further back – long, long ago, thousands of lives and years to the very start, to the conception of all conceptions. To a time when birth and death were one, and all reality was held in the hand of the Prime Mover of all.

And the seer tumbled fitfully into sleep, rolling his head from side to side as he waited for a deeper sleep to come to him, and finally it came. Sweet dreamless slumber rocked his soul gently in the night. And he felt as if he were being lifted from his body, as if he were being cradled in great green arms, wanted and warm, untroubled and calm. Becoming part of a greater being, becoming absorbed into a soft haven of happiness, where his anguished knowledge became a gift rather than a burden, where his pain was taken from his soul with a smile. Then there came a great silence and he dreamed no more.

The seer with his dreams and fancies.

THE HEALER

AND she was the healer with her herbs and hidden learning. Her lore was the uppermost branch of a mighty tree with its roots buried deep in the soil of centuries. She travelled the land in all weathers dispensing her cures to all who needed her ministrations. There was a holiness about her as she journeyed with her great pack of roots and flowers and leaves upon her back. She was old, or she seemed old, so wrinkled was her face with its deep eyes filled with wisdom and sorrow, and her shoulders so bent with the weight of her burden.

Once she had a donkey to carry her prescriptions, a grey soft creature of prodigious strength. She had thought that he had loved her until one night she had left him untethered, and he had run off with the wild ponies. She saw him yet in her mind's eye as he galloped off into the dusk, braying his farewell as he went, with not a backward glance. And she often wondered about the sterile offspring of his precarious couplings.

And once too, there had been a man who travelled the roads with her. Long, long ago in the springtime of her trade, he had joined with her in her own mating, and all that she had from that relationship was the wasting sickness and a stillborn child buried in the mists of the past. And the man had also run off in the night, running off to the wild women who inhabited the ravaged towns that stood stark and dark against the setting sun. And she would like awake at night and think of him and weep for his soul, for now he must be long dead.

Now though, she lay on a bed of mint, rue and camomile, and her eyes were blessed with a sound and dreamless sleep. But when she woke she still had to travel the desolate roads, she still had to see the sights, the ruins, the rusted metal heaving from the earth. She had to see the results of the disasters that had occurred in the long ago, when man had not the will to repair the destruction, and her old eyes could not comprehend the whys and wherefores of the shrouded past.

And she came to small gatherings of people as she went, sick ailing folk who lived in roughly hewn stone barns and tilled the unwilling soil for nourishment. And she gave them her medicines, she offered acorns for looseness of the bowels, agrimony for coughs, and the holy thistle with its grey-green leaves for sneezing and running noses. And they would offer her food in return, but she refused them, preferring food of her own preparation. She ate naught but roots and herbs and fish that she had gathered on her way. For she knew that there were beneficial to her own long-standing illness. She would sit alone in a corner watching her patients with a secret smile upon her lips before taking her leave of them. And she would walk on along that same path she followed each and every year.

Alone at night she would stare out across the almost treeless vista and wonder how long her store of medicines would last, for the earth seemed to grow more barren with each passing season, and the collecting grew still more difficult for her aging bones. But there was a place she knew, a still green place, tended with love by generations of givers, not despoiled by takers. And each year at this time she would go there, she would tarry awhile, knowing that in that place there was a day when the sun would shine, a day when there was joy in the air, and a memory of other joys that had gone before. It seemed to be untouched by time, unimpaired by the follies of mankind. And she would go there and talk with the people who dwelt in the ancient wood.

The healer of the sick would spend her day with the keepers of the soil, and together they would touch the atmosphere attempting to return to the land that which had been taken from it. She would quietly gather her comfrey, her honeysuckle and her alder, and make her preparations. Ointments and potions would fill her pack, and in payment she would give them seeds that she had found along her way. And they would smile and watch the earth moving with delight.

This year, though, there seemed to be an urgency in the air, a gentle compulsion filled her steps. It seemed to her as if her ailments were falling from her as she walked, she felt young again, her pack weightless. And there was spring in her as she started to run, to race headlong down the road that led to an evergreen clearing in a timeless wood, with her cape and hair streaming out behind her.

And she was the healer with her herbs and hidden learning.

THE MEETING

AND he was the watcher in the night, skulking like a leper amid the stars. An air of utter desolation hung about him as he idled within his lost corner. For he knew that he had altered the shape of creation, he had been made aware that his unwanted incursion into a minor patch of spinning debris had started a chain of events, the results of which could not be foreseen, would not perhaps, become apparent until the inner and outer universes merged and became as one. And then, joined together, they would journey on to the final cataclysmic melding with that which lay beyond the imagination of even the prime mover of the first eternity.

But what the watcher in the night had perpetrated, was sufficient to disfigure the unity of the cosmic order. There was now a flaw in the astral palace, a blemish upon the face of the constellations. And he lurked in the endless night with guilt pouring from him like the prayers of an abandoned penitent. Sometimes, in his dreams, he would revisit the scene of his innocent crime and wonder how it had all occurred. He had not meant any harm, he had hoped for glory but what remained was the dross of unfulfilled ambition. And he could not change a thing, his grief was merely a reflection of the frustration of the futility of the fallible.

And he would walk the deserts, the hills and the oceans, berating himself for his impotence. Till one time he came upon a small area of trees which glowed like a green furnace, and wondered that he had not noticed it before. He moved

THE MAN IN GREEN

the trees aside to peer within, to see standing there a figure of brilliant verdure, spilling energy into the heavens. The two creatures looked at each other, and for one brief moment there was silence, it was like a catch in the throat of creation as time stood still, the world stopped its turning and the clouds ceased their shifting through the blue heaven. The green fire and the tears of the watcher in the night were suspended as the two surveyed each other before speaking. "Who are you?" the watcher asked, "that I have never seen you in this lost world". The man in green answered. "You have never seen me for I do not exist in the reality of time, I am merely a figment of the imagination of humanity. I was created out of his need for me". "Why then", the watcher replied, "do I see you now?" "It is that the same mankind who originated me, who then abandoned me, which now has the greatest need of my being. They now have need for my physical aid, rather than the gentle persuasiveness of my subconscious actuality". "How can you know this thing?" said the watcher, "why is it that this should be the moment for your manifestation?" "Before I answer you, perhaps I should tell you of this race of beings I serve and why they have been brought so low to be then raised so high".

The watcher in the night nodded, and sat beside the man in green in the grove, feeling the grass, still against his hand. And the man in green told him of mankind from the beginning, how he had been savage, then noble, then savage again. He told stories of humanity's quest for holiness and righteousness, but how every time it seemed that they would achieve greatness, the greed and selfishness that seemed to be born within them would drag them back from the pinnacle.

ASHES OF THE FAIR

He spoke of the other times and in other guises that he had walked among them. And how eagerly they had listened to his words, but how quickly they had forgotten after he had left them. It had seemed that they could not bear to accept guidance from an outside source. The creation of wisdom had to appear to emanate from within the soul of man, otherwise it had no value, and they twisted his words to their own ends until it became almost unrecognisable from the original.

The he told of the devil that had been created to give man an excuse for his own shortcomings, a tempter to implant thoughts into the mind, like seeds, to flourish in hidden recesses. He then went on to tell of mankind's thrust for the stars, whilst using artefacts that paved the way to its own doom, the poisons that filled the air, the rain that ruined the trees, that destroyed the land, that defiled the soil, that sapped the energies of the firmament. "And now we are left with this", he said, as he held his hand over the landscape, "an almost barren planet, with perhaps this one last opportunity to realise its reason for existence". "Why have you continued to serve such ungrateful masters?" asked the watcher, "surely there was to be a greater reward than despair?"

The man in green smiled. "Ah yes", he mused "there was always the hope, the belief that the greatness that walked hand in hand with the stupidity would one day assert itself, allowing the beauty that was in the soul of man to flood forth and enrich the earth". And then he spoke to his alien guest of the music and the poetry, the creativity that the species was capable of. He talked of art and literature and love. He talked of flowers and forests and great ships that plied the seas gathering knowledge and riches. "There was so much that was good

THE MAN IN GREEN

among them", he went on, "and yet so much evil, there were times when I was unable to tell whether the creatures I was created to serve were gods themselves, or merely fornicating, killing machines".

Then he sighed and rubbed his shadowed eyes, as if wiping away a tear, before he continued. "They could not comprehend the simplicity of life, everything became complicated or secretive, even the messages that were passed down to them by their forefathers became ciphers, obscure codes that could only be interpreted by self-interest". "Why did you not force them to understand, to listen to you, before it was too late?" asked the watcher, "perhaps then all the bloodshed and suffering could have been avoided".

The man in green looked at his visitor, to see from his visage that he would have compelled them to do his bidding. He smiled again. "No, that is not the way, you cannot use compulsion as a weapon, for therein lies the road to irrevocable disaster, there would always be a seed of doubt in the mind of the coerced. They must come with free will and joy". The watcher threw back his head and laughed, the sound echoing around the stillness of the timeless glade.

"Come now", he said, "look about this accursed world of yours, the people are sick, they are hungry, they do not possess the skills to claw their way to salvation. The disaster of which you speak has already occurred. "Perhaps you are right", the man in green replied, "but it was not irrevocable, for the memory of humanity has now been cleansed of impurities, and the time I have been waiting for has arrived, and even now they are coming to me, coming for help and guidance, my call has gone out across all the lands, and they are flooding in as once they did, and I am ready for them".

The watcher in the night stood shaking his head. "You are wrong, green man, you have forgotten their devil . . . . ."

"No, they have forgotten him".

"They forgot you and yet you still exist".

"But I must still try for them, there must be hope for their future".

"Of course there is hope, but there must also be fear, for that is the way of creation".

And the man in green bowed his head for a moment, and when he looked again, his visitor had gone. And the watcher in the night hovered in the heavens, aware now of his purpose, and why he had been drawn inexorably to this small patch of dust that meandered through the Milky Way. His hopes for mankind were not malign, they were just different. "Perhaps", he smiled, "I am the forgotten devil of their youth". He shrugged. "Perhaps not, nevertheless, I shall stay and watch for a while". And he hangs there, skulking like a leper amid the stars.

THE SIGHTLESS CHILD

AND she was the child with her recollections of the sights of summer. There was a time once when her eyes could look out upon the world, sparkling with life and light. Gradually though, her days faded into a perpetual night. For her there was naught but the flashes of half-remembered colours, that sparked when she pressed her lids together as she turned her empty eyes toward the shining sun or to the blazing fire as it crackled beneath the stars. And she felt the world with the tips of her fingers, heard it with her ears. She followed her family by the sounds they made or by the smell of their clothes, she stopped when they did, and helped to prepare the food by the almost bat-like senses that had developed since her curtains had been drawn.

And she knew it was night by the cold in the wind and the aromas on the air. Then she would lie upon her blanket shrouded in her special solitude, listening to the noises of the darkness, personal sounds that were beyond the reach of the others, she would listen to the gentle snores and the breathing of her brothers and sisters, and hear in surprise, the sudden passion filled moans of her parents. And she would move away, feeling with her feet the soil or grass beneath her. She loved the night, it gave her equality and independence as she walked. There were times, too, when the night gave her superiority. It was when the moon was hidden behind the clouds, when the mists swirled in from the sea, and when the vision of the sighted was obscured, they would turn to her.

ASHES OF THE FAIR

They would need the special instincts of the blind child to lead them, to find the hidden paths that led them away from the terrifying nocturnal howlings of the untamed creatures of darkness.

And there was one time when she led them to a ruined town, deserted for centuries, crumbled away to its foundations. It stood, or rather it crouched, fearful of further destruction in the midst of the wasted wilderness. They gave no thought of what it might have been in the long distant past, they merely lit a fire beside the remnants of a wall and prepared their food, which was eaten in a desultory silence before they wrapped themselves in their blankets and slept.

But the unseeing child did not sleep, she waited awhile listening to the breathing of her family till it grew heavy, then she rose and walked off to explore the town. She stumbled through the night, feeling the dust and weeds beneath her, and the hard cold of the broken concrete that had splintered against the might of time. She walked with her hands stretched out before her and listened to the noises of the night as she went. She heard the sudden scurrying sounds of rats in the debris, and the beating wings of the blind bat flying to roost in its decayed attic. There was the hum or buzz of thousands of night insects eating their way through rotted timbers, withered by years of indifference.

Suddenly she fell as she walked into a wall that barred her path, it was smooth, not rough and worn like the others, it felt strange to her sensitive fingertips. She sniffed, but the aroma of decay did not emanate from this wall as it did from the rest. She moved along it feeling its surface, it was metal, but like no metal she had ever felt. Once it had been the foundation of a mighty tower reaching up to the sky, but she could not know that as she circled it. Could not comprehend its purpose or fate as she sat feeling the cool smoothness against the thin fabric of her garment as she leant her back against it.

She reached out her hand in the darkness to feel an odd metal cylinder at the base of the wall, she drew it toward her and examined it with her hands. It was almost three hands high and the thickness of her thigh. She put her nose to it but there was only the odour of the earth clinging to it. She twisted it and turned it, to find eventually that it possessed a movable top. She took it off and inserted her curious hand with a degree of trepidation and removed the contents. There was a paper with pictures upon its surface, there was one of a man shouting to a crowd with his arms waving in the air, another one of a weeping woman, there was a third that showed a black man shaking hands with a white man. And around the picture were black marks, some large and some small. Had she education she could have read the words, understood the pictures, had she the sight.

She discarded the paper, it was inedible. It was caught by the breeze and blown away into the debris of the town. She inserted her hand again and removed a plastic article, which she forced open with her sharp fingernails, she had never felt plastic, it was hard and brittle, but she broke it and drew out a long thin ribbon of tape. She could not know that the voices of the past were on that tape as it wrapped itself around the branches of a dead tree and waved weirdly in the wind, like ghostly tendrils of blighted ambition. Had she had machinery she could have played that tape, could have heard the message of hope of a better world for the children. She could have heard the music and songs, the poetry, the laughter, but she discarded it too, and searched again. There were more pictures which she cast aside, small metal discs with the carved head of a woman on one side, they made a pleasant chinking sound as she rattled them, but she could not eat them and abandoned them in their turn.

Suddenly she realised that the sounds had changed, it was daybreak and she must return to her family. She rose, and in doing so, knocked the canister on to its side, spilling out the rest of its contents on to the ground, to be rained upon and rotted by the future, to be blown into dust by the winds of tomorrow. And forgotten by the blind child who stumbled back the way she had come. And there was a different feeling to the day, she felt the excitement rising in her blood, she could not describe it, new colours filled her mind as she urged her family on. They could not feel it, but it was there. She was being drawn on, and they for once were following in her wake. They could not see or feel and yet the sun was shining, their eyes were open, they could comprehend the clouds, the grass, the road beneath their feet, yet they were unable to visualise that which she saw with her inner sight, and beating within her brain, like a great bell, was a voice that beseeched her on.

"Blind child with your lifeless eyes,

Lead them in your sightless, sinless footsteps".

And they grasped the hem of her garment so as to maintain the pace of the child as she sped along the road.

The child with her recollections of the sights of summer.

THE HARVESTER

AND he was the harvester, the man who tilled the soil and protected the land. His line stretched back a thousand lifetimes to the dawn of time, and he was the last of the generations of man who had the guardianship of the holy glade. Over the years the area of the glade had been diminished by the ravages of the passage of time. Where it had once stretched as far as the eyes could see, filled with trees and flowers, with shrubs and herbs and growing food, it now nestled alone in a tiny valley, sheltered on three sides by great rolling hills, the fourth side was open to the sun and to the river that flowed like a silver arrow through the heart of the remaining woodland.

Around the valley a wall of wood had been erected to protect the small band of men and women within from the depredations of the outside world. How long the wall had existed, no one knew, but it had been built centuries earlier by the ancestors of the harvester at a time when the animals began to run wild. When the insanity in their blood and on their teeth filled man with terror, and wild-eyed madness. And the vale survived behind its wall, plants germinated, bloomed, filling the air with gentle aromas of an earlier time. It was a soft life, a peace was abroad in the breeze. The rain that had destroyed the land beyond had not touched the glade, the trees still bore their fruits and shed their leaves in their season. Feeding the earth, dead leaves upon thankful soil, nourishing the ground. Dead trees upon dead trees time out of mind nurturing nature, a spark of life that flowed through the veins of the valley in an

ASHES OF THE FAIR

unbroken line whose beginning was found at the birth of the man in green.

And the river that ran clear and pure through the woodland came untouched and unsullied from a deep well at the centre of the earth, and it too fed the land, it sustained the fish that swam silver and gold in the clear rippling waters. And the people drank of the water and thrived, there was an air of enchantment in the wind, a timelessness about them as they went about their daily tasks, and the sun smiled down upon their endeavours.

And the man in green dwelt there also, and he smiled too upon them, for here he knew was the core of the future, people living in harmony with the elements, speaking peace to one another without jealousy, without cupidity, without selfishness. And the man in green remembered a child long, long ago, who had played innocently in the sand and who had listened to his voice echoing in his mind, and the face of the child was reflected in the faces of the inhabitants of the woods, and the eyes of the child were the eyes of the harvester.

And the man in green watched as the harvester walked through the trees, examining them, encouraging them in their growth, talking soft words to them as he passed. He walked along the line of the wooden wall as he went that all was in order, he waved greetings to those he passed and sang as he went, a small new song for the new day. And he knew that this was a special day as he walked to the top of the hill and looked down upon the woodland, an emerald jewel in the heart of the wilderness. Then suddenly, as he watched, his heart surged as the trees seemed to explode with a green fire spilling out into the still morning. And his eyes widened as the colours filled

THE MAN IN GREEN

him with green brilliance, and he shuddered with delight at the variation of the display.

A special day, he thought as he descended the slopes of the hill to see the people with their faces filled with wonder, but what does it mean? And he led them all back to the summit so as to better see the colours, and they clapped their hands with joy and incredulity as they watched. And behind them the countryside was filled with tiny specks of moving humanity, faster and faster they came until the land was covered with the mass, and the Harvester walked again to the foot of the hill and began to tear down the wooden wall that had been their protection for so long. And he still knew not why, the Harvester who tilled the soil and protected the land.

THE MAN IN GREEN

AND he was the man in green who had survived the perdition of mankind. Years becoming lifetimes becoming centuries, time passing, world changing, even the golden shining stars had shifted in their courses as he waited. And the moment was now. He was the recorder, and naught had escaped his searching eye as year had followed weary year. His infinite mind had retained all that had occurred. He had registered the rises to glory and the plunges to extinction of countless empires. And he alone knew the reasons for their collapse.

Long, so long ago, man had turned from him and he had waited with endless patience for the time when they would return, of their own volition, to his side. And the moment was now. And he was the guardian of the soul of humanity, he had held it against all evil, against all temptation. He kept it in trust for them, pristine and pure, in the heart of his green sanctuary. Once the soul of mankind had been as perfect, but time and greed had despoiled the individual quintessence of the race. And the man in green had waited for the time to arrive when the repairs could be made to the soul of man.

And the moment was now. He stood amid the green fire spraying the atmosphere with a riot of colour, and watched them as they approached his glade, as once they had done in the past. They were a little apprehensive, startled by the blaze of variegated hues. He saw them as they stood in their hundreds, humbly by his trees, waiting. Waiting for they knew not what. And he saw faces that he recognised from the ashes

THE MAN IN GREEN

of history. Here was the reborn face of a long-dead crone, with the shadow of an ancient kiss still upon her cheek. And there was the valiant, wrinkled visage of an unknown dwarf who had stumbled in beauty from hardship to hardship, from peril to peril. He saw the features of a crippled man reflected in the light that emanated from the eyes of a longed-for friend. And he heard the voice of a troubadour, the cry of an acrobat. And he saw the desperate searching eyes of a frantic woman seeking the truth, he saw the lost and pleading eyes of a preacher who had abandoned his dreams.

They were all here now, faces from the past become signposts towards tomorrow. Reborn souls that had haunted the corridors and highways of history, and the man in green wept with the joy and mingled sadness that filled his being. There was so much to tell them, so many mistakes to correct. He wanted to tell them of sharing, that there should be an equality in creation. He wanted them to learn about love, that it should be a giving thing, and the delight of love should be found in the acceptance of the gift of the bestower. And he would teach them of simplicity, that they would come to realise that truth is the property of all, not a mystic entity that is held only in the hands of those that are able to interpret it as they see fit.

Truth is unchanging, therefore the illumination of it should shine unaltered by the variations of time. He would show them that the greatest responsibility of humanity is to be found in his defence of nature, to take from the world no more than the world has to offer. And to return to the soil and to the seas an equal abundance of riches. And he wanted to show them that their growth, both spiritual and intellectual could be accomplished without pain, it would be a gentle blossoming, slowly waxing as does the oak in its seasons to glory. They would also learn that in a million years of recorded and unrecorded history, death and war had achieved naught but despair and bitterness.

And he looked at their expectant expressions, alive with the reflected radiance, and watched as a bronze coloured girl moved, bewildered, from the depths of the crowd. And the glade was silent, desperately silent, as she stood before his majestic tree looking up beyond its ancient branches, her eyes were dazzled by the green fire that stretched high into the clouds, spurting out like great arms of liquid jade that seemed to fill the heavens with the reflection of its power. And there was a mighty gasp, a great fading sigh, when the flames, having reached to their furthest possible range and yet still be comprehensible to the crowd, suddenly stood still for a small pulsating moment before plunging back into the heart of the glade. And all was still.

Then silently, imperceptibly, the man in green stepped from the depths of the trees. He seemed to float across the grass, and the air was filled with his inaudible laughter. The gathering watched as he moved, scarcely able to believe what they saw, but their eyes were wide with joy and wonder. And he stood at last before the bronze-coloured girl and placed his green hand upon her brow, and she too laughed with him at the touch. And the joy spread around the glade, electric laughter filled the day, great spasms of uncontrollable delight. Then it fell silent again as the man in green and the bronze-coloured girl seemed to flicker, to shimmer against the background of

Edwards Brothers Malloy
Oxnard, CA USA
December 13, 2013

THE MAN IN GREEN

the trees as the two of them merged and parted like the dancing flames of a fire, then finally they were one.

And where once there had been a girl and a deity, there now stood before the astonished crowd, a tall girl. A fair girl in a gown of brilliant white whose golden tresses cascaded about her shoulders. And she walked towards them with her hands open before her in supplication. And she began to speak in a soft tone, a gentle persuasive sound that filled the day with truth, and the world with relief.

And the watcher in the night surveyed it all from his temple in the skies, and wondered where it would all end.

ISBN 141208637-X